A MODERN

CHRISTMAS CAROL

by

KEVIN FLANAGAN

Copyright © 2024 Kevin Flanagan.
All Rights Reserved

No part of this publication may be reproduced, distributed, or transmitted in any form, or by any means, including photocopying, recording, or other electronic or mechanical, methods without the prior written permission of the author, except in the case of brief quotations embodied in reviews and certain other non-commercial uses permitted by copyright law.

Dedication

To my friend Paul McGlade

(1955-2024)

Acknowledgements:

To Ciaran, Maria, Kuba & Maya, Mairead, Anne and Catherine and all the family in Tunbridge Wells for their continuous support.

To the Order of Malta's Knight Run Homeless outreach, where this story had its origins.

To Laurence O'Bryan, Zeynep and Robert for their weekly support (and sustenance!)

To Dylan Townsend for his encouragement and feedback

To dear Cara and her wonderful family in Udon Thani.

To Diamond my best pal in BK!

To Salilla Atikarnbodee and all at the Salil Hotel Riverside Bangkok for her generous support while I was finishing the book

To Phil Kelly & Anne Flanagan for their support over the years.

And to AK and Padraig for always being there in fitness and in health!

And finally to Charles Dickens for creating one of the world's greatest stories and inspiring me to reinvent what is probably the first telling of a NDE (Near Death Experience).

Kevin Flanagan Dublin, Ireland 2024

Why I wrote this book:
I first played Ebenezer Scrooge in a street theatre production in January, 2018. The next year I adapted the book and produced and directed a stage version of A Christmas Carol for a homeless charity I volunteered for: The Knights Run.

We put it on in an old Victorian hall in the HQ of the Order of Malta in Dublin and it was a great success. I played Scrooge and loved the role and the ghostly inspired journey of redemption it portrayed. We staged two more stage productions in 2021 & 2022, raising tens of thousands for the homeless charity.

I also wrote a film script setting A Christmas Carol in modern times with Scrooge as a property billionaire. We made a short film of that (link here) and wrote a full screenplay and out of those came this book.

Why do I love Ebenezer Scrooge's tale of redemption?

It is such a profound story showing us the world of spirit and morality that I believe surrounds us. A world in which our actions have consequences that will determine our fate in the next world.

I hope you enjoy this modern retelling of this Charles Dickens classic. I wrote it to bring the story to a modern, younger audience but the original themes remain the same. Especially the main theme: that we treat our fellow human beings with respect and selfless love.

Kevin Flanagan Dublin, 2024

Part 1 –

Ebenezer Scrooge –

The Ruthless Billionaire

1

The old man looked terrified. A bead of sweat trickled down his brow and onto his nose and dangled there, like a raindrop catching the light. A shiver ran through the old man's body at the sound of a door closing above him, followed by footsteps descending. The drop of sweat fell to the ground as the old man's head swivelled and his eyes looked up and took in the approaching figure. Tall and stiff, the newcomer was dressed all in black. Black homburg hat. Black suit and tie. A long, tailored overcoat. Black shoes polished so bright they reflected the light. The tall man could have been an undertaker, such was his sombre air and dark clothing. Only the educated eye recognised the glittering Patek Philippe watch, and the austere cut of the Armani suit and overcoat. Garments and accessories beyond the means and taste of most undertakers.

The old man doffed his chauffeur's hat as he opened the door of the enormous limousine. But the austere man did not get in. Instead, his hawk eyes were fixed unhappily on a battered old Mercedes Benz. Once it had been a classic, a rare 1957 Mercedes Ponton. But the years had taken their toll and it looked decidedly down-at-the-heel, as it rested next to the tradesman's entrance of the palatial house, its glorious bodywork now covered in a patina of rust. The hawk eyes of the tall man prised themselves away from the old car and held the chauffeur in a blink-less stare.

"What is my father's old car doing here?"

"Mr Scrooge, I was going to drive it away the moment I finished work."

"You were going to drive it? Where exactly?"

The old man cleared his throat nervously. "To my house, Mr Scrooge. It's my last day at work."

A pregnant pause. "And why would you be taking my father's old car?" The ice-blue eyes could have cut a diamond. In this case they seemed to cut off the old man's air supply, as words formed on cracked lips but failed to emerge. A plume of red appeared on the skin at the old man's neck, spreading rapidly above the starched white collar of his shirt. "Mr—" he gulped, then taking a shallow breath, he tried again. "Mr Scrooge, you may remember your father gave me the car before he passed away. He said it would be my retirement gift."

The icy blue eyes continued to regard the chauffeur as a bird of prey might regard a mouse.

"Retirement?" said the tall figure through a forced smile.

"Yes, sir. Fifty years of service ends today."

"And my father promised you his old car?"

The old man's smile dared to appear, mixed with a generous dollop of pride.

"Yes, Mr Scrooge. You know how I love to tinker with old cars..."

Another long pause. The unblinking eyes narrowed. "And the keys?"

The old man fished in his pockets, the red patch on his neck spreading. He held up a trembling hand. An antique leather fob with faded gold lettering bearing the logo Mercedes Benz caught the morning sunshine.

"Did I and my late father always pay you well for your services, George?" Scrooge asked.

The old chauffeur nodded; the red blotch was now creeping up his cheeks.

"Surely that should be enough?" said Mr Scrooge, taking the keys. "Sadly, my father was always more generous with everyone but his son."

A glacial smile touched his austere lips but did not reach his eyes as he pocketed the keys. The eyes of George, meanwhile, had pooled with two large tears. He stood stock still for a moment, his quivering lips moving wordlessly.

Scrooge observed him, his face twisting into a look of pure disgust. He sucked in his breath and stooping, entered the limo and settled on the backseat, picking the neatly folded *Financial Times* that lay there ready for him. He opened up the pink pages as if to shield himself from his chauffeur's crass display of emotion.

George paused for a moment before shutting the passenger door with a soft thud. He shuffled back to the driver's door, his old, cracked lips mouthing words impossible to comprehend. He sat in the driver's seat and with a great effort of will, started the engine. The car moved up the wide gravel drive and onto the road. George forced his bloodshot eyes not to look at the old Mercedes that, up until seconds ago, had been his.

He stifled a sob.

2

They had barely gone fifty metres when the stretch limo braked to a sudden halt. Jolted upright, Scrooge lowered his paper to see what the delay was. A small crowd of well-heeled residents were gathered on the road outside the mediaeval church that stood next to Scrooge's mansion. They were watching as a stream of choir boys and girls crossed the road and gathered in the eaves of the church. The last boy and girl carried the infant Jesus in a wicker basket. The strains of the Christmas carol *Silent Night* filled the air, while a young vicar, dressed in a gaudy Christmas jumper, conducted his young choir with one hand, while shaking the alms box with the other. The alms box bore the message HELP OUR REFUGEES.

"Drive on!" Scrooge commanded, his voice edged with anger and George obediently revved the stationary car. But no one moved and the road remained blocked. Scrooge, cursing under his breath, lowered the window and, sticking his head out, barked, "Move there!"

Hostile glances met Scrooge but the crowd moved slowly and reluctantly onto the pavement. The young vicar, however, on seeing the limo, hurried over, proffering his alms box and smiling desperately.

"Ah, Mr Scrooge – a donation for our Christmas carol fund—"

The request was silenced as the electric window closed on the vicar's outstretched hand. Scrooge, a satisfied smile on his face, resumed reading his paper. The vicar looked on, the smile still fixed desperately as the limo picked up speed. Scrooge lowered his paper and glanced back at the hapless vicar, still standing in the road, his alms box outstretched.

"Everyone's on the make," Scrooge said, loud enough for the chauffeur to hear. But old George did not respond. His face, which had broken out in a faint smile at the sight of the children, was sad once more. He dared not look at his boss. Instead, he glanced up as a shard of light caught his attention. A speck, silver and bright cutting across the cold, blue Christmas Eve sky. Was it a plane? A satellite? A rocket? The old chauffeur continued to stare at the fascinating light until a horn blast brought him back to Earth. The great limo had drifted across the road and an oncoming truck was forced to swerve, honking George in the process.

"For God's sake!" Scrooge's sharp words stung George's neck. Cold beads of sweat prickled his brow as he regained control and steered the vehicle back to his side of the road.

"Sorry, sir," he muttered. Minutes later, as they arrived at Westminster Bridge, he glanced up again. But the light had disappeared, the sky now covered by dull, grey clouds.

Will it snow on Christmas Day? George wondered. For once, the prospect did not fill him with joy. All he could see was his battered old Mercedes lying beneath a blanket of white snow, neglected, unwanted. An involuntary shudder ran through his old, bent body. He did not deserve this, not at the ripe old age of seventy. His encounter with Scrooge that morning had heralded the death of the only thing he was looking forward to in his retirement. He discreetly brushed away a tear as his mind wandered back to Scorpius Scrooge, the father of the man sitting in the back of the limo. Father and son were different in every way possible. George had served Scorpius Scrooge for many years and in all that time he had never experienced such cruelty as from the son Ebenezer.

George felt tears well in his eyes again. He tried to master himself. He would not lose his self-respect on the last day of work. George glanced back at his master. The austere figure was still using the pink newspaper sheets as a shield. And for a long moment George pondered why Scrooge Junior had decided not to honour his father's wishes. It had nothing to do with money. Ebenezer Scrooge was one of the wealthiest men in Britain, if not the world. No, Ebenezer had used the opportunity to insult his long-dead father.

And a question formed in George's mind: what must Scorpius Scrooge have done to make his only son hate him so much?

3

As the limousine carrying Ebenezer Scrooge skirted the dark flowing waters of the Thames, a young six-year-old girl was waiting in the long queue in front of St. Paul's Cathedral to visit the crib. She was holding the hand of her mother and playing hopscotch on the spot, jumping rhythmically from one foot to the other. She did this both to relieve the boredom and to keep warm as the temperature plummeted below zero. And as she double-jumped and turned, she caught sight of something that made her stop dead in her tracks. Her face angled up to the sky, where she saw something glittering beside the dome of Sir Christopher Wren's masterpiece.

The little girl stood transfixed, her large pupils narrowing as they focused on the shard of light that seemed suspended in the air above. It was not an aeroplane, she was sure of that. It did not move like a plane. Indeed, it was a light so clear and bright that it seemed to speak to her. Then she understood and tugged urgently at her mother's hand. "Ma – the Star of Bethlehem!"

At first the mother did not look down, so engaged was she with chatting on her mobile phone. It took two more tugs before she looked in the direction where her daughter pointed. "Sorry, love, what?"

"The Star of Bethlehem, Ma!"

The mother wrinkled her eyes. All she could see was the cold blue sky. "There, Ma – don't you see it?"

Other faces were craning up but they too only had blank stares. Perhaps her little girl was imagining it, the mother thought, scanning the sky in vain. After all, her daughter had been in the school Christmas play that week, where the Star of Bethlehem had been played by her friend Debbie. Strange what a child's imagination could do, she thought, stroking the little girl's head while resuming her phone call.

Across the river, on the opposite bank, a rare peregrine falcon was perched near the top of the giant, disused chimney that dominated the Tate Modern museum. The peregrine's large eyes, one of the most powerful lenses in the animal kingdom, suddenly fixed on an object above. Unblinkingly, they followed the same shard of light and on an impulse the bird of prey took off, soaring upwards, cartwheeling in what looked like a dance of pure delight. And still the light crossed the sky, visible to some, invisible to others. Soon it was above London's docklands, where another set of eyes looked up and stared intently.

4

These eyes belonged to a young man. But on closer examination, the eyes seemed strained and exhausted. After a long moment, a smile appeared on the young man's face. A face, in truth, that looked far older than his years. He had been following the light in the sky for an hour now. It had led him over a bridge and along the great river and now it appeared to hover motionless above him. Or was he imagining the whole thing? He ran a sleeve across his sweating brow. He was shaking but not from the cold. It was as if some fever gripped him. He closed his eyes and yet still saw the light dancing through his eyelids. Or was he imagining that as well? He felt himself sway on his feet. It was time to rest before he fell over.

The man sat down on the cold flagstones directly under where the light shone and placed the leather satchel he was carrying beside him. He looked along the cold, paved pedestrian walkway that hugged the side of the River Thames. Above him towered office blocks, all glinting glass and steel in the cold morning sunshine. Most, he could see, were empty on this Christmas Eve. Only the odd security staff member manning a desk at reception. Otherwise, the buildings were as quiet and empty as the streets.

The young man sighed and, pulling open his satchel, took out a brightly coloured handkerchief and laid it on the ground. He then proceeded to take out small objects that glinted in the morning sunshine and arranged them on the fabric. For anyone coming across the scene, the young man looked strangely out of place. His dark skin hinted at origins in a warmer clime. The long, dark braided hair in stark contrast to the usual slick city gent that frequented these byways. This young man wore a type of bombachas or gaucho pants, with a poncho over a white shirt, and a wide leather hat shielding the eyes from the bright morning sun. This impression of a man from a more exotic place was reinforced by the collection of handmade jewellery that he was laying out in front of him. Anyone who had visited the rainforests of Central America would have recognised these artefacts: green, rhyolite jasper beads, braided bracelets, a rare green rainforest gemstone pendant. Necklaces made with soft, supple leather, the centrepiece a semi-precious stone in the colours of amethyst and lapis lazuli. But these did not match the silver locket that hung around the young man's neck. This was decidedly antique and European. And this anomaly would have struck anyone versed in the crafts. For the young man's hands often came up to touch and caress the silver locket, as if it gave comfort to him. As if to reinforce the point, the young man cupped the silver locket in both hands while looking directly up at the shard of light and mouthing silent words, like a prayer, before turning his attention back to the items laid out on the brightly coloured cloth. He took out a folded piece of cardboard and propped it beside the jewellery. It was roughly written and said: FOR SALE – HANDMADE!

Anyone passing would have looked at the young man slumping exhausted on the cold flagstones beside the River Thames and wondered what on Earth he was doing there on this freezing Christmas Eve. Was he working? Broke? A homeless refugee? A tourist? A combination of all? The homeless option seemed most likely, as the young man's appearance showed definite signs of neglect. His hair had a dank, unhealthy look. There was a pallor to his dark, sunken cheeks that spoke of malnourishment, while the bloodshot eyes hinted at a distinct lack of sleep. Finally, the onlooker would have been struck by a distinct look of sadness that seemed to shadow the otherwise handsome face. But for a moment, all that sadness and care seemed suspended as the young man tilted his head to gaze at the light in the sky. The eyes of the young man were not dark brown, but as blue as the sky above. And these eyes again caressed the shard of light. The light that had led him to that exact spot. And this time, when the young man clasped the silver locket, it sprung open, revealing a faded photo inside, a photo of a young man and a woman kissing.

"Mamãe," the young man whispered, his eyes moist as he looked at the two faded faces, gently touching the surface of the photo with the top of his index finger, a finger that was ingrained with dirt. His young eyes caressing the image of the woman with great tenderness.

"Oi!" A sharp, ugly shout filled the air and the look of quiet wonder vanished as the young face looked at four men that seemed to have come out of thin air and now surrounded him. It was not so much their tightly cropped heads, Doc Martens boots, or tight-fitting designer jeans that made his heart suddenly pound in his chest, but something else. Something permeating the air around them, like a cloud of brooding violence. He did not rise to meet the four men standing over him. Instead, with a trembling hand, he began gathering up his jewellery. But as he did this, an ugly voice cracked the air.

"What are you doing here?"

"En hao entendo inglês," the young man said, carefully replacing the jewellery in his satchel. His voice was thin, that of a teenager yet to achieve full maturity. And suddenly he looked very vulnerable.

"Don't speak English?" another voice snarled. No answer.

"What are you doing here if you don't speak English?"

The young man finally stood up, repeating the phrase, "En hao entendo inglês." He was tall, much taller than the four that surrounded him, but painfully thin.

One of the youths stepped forward and shoved the young man in the chest. "Speak English!"

Another shove, this more powerful, and the young man staggered backwards. The loud cry of a swooping seagull warned him that he was getting near the edge of the quayside. And there was no protective railing, only a thirty-foot drop into the River Thames.

"You hear me, mate?" said the same angry voice. Another shove and the young man tripped backwards over an iron stanchion. A stanchion that had been preserved from the time, long, long ago, when sailboats secured their ropes to it when docking to unload their cargo. This symbol of another age became the young man's downfall – literally. He felt a sharp stab of pain in his Achilles tendon as he toppled over the cold iron. Suddenly, he found himself looking up at the sky and at the silver locket that seemed suddenly suspended in the air above him. For a split second, it felt like he was flying. Then he hit the freezing water and was engulfed in darkness.

5

In one of the tall office blocks that looked over the River Thames, a woman also happened to be looking at the bright light that hung suspended in the cold morning sky.

Bobbi Cratchit was a woman in her mid-thirties but one who looked far older. To an outside observer, it looked as if a younger, prettier woman had been lost beneath years of care. Her long, black, unbrushed hair showed the first strands of grey. Strands that had gone untreated. Her once pretty face, devoid of any make-up, showed wrinkles and care lines around her mouth and eyes – eyes that were ringed with dark smudges. Her clothes showed similar signs of neglect. The dark blue cardigan was worn thin at the elbows, while the starched white cotton shirt was fraying around the collar. The fingernails of the woman were bitten and chipped. But it was her eyes that told the saddest story. They were eyes that seemed to have lost their lustre and sheen. They were dull and lifeless, as if some great trouble or care had sucked the life out of them. But the troubled look had been temporarily put on hold as she gazed up at the bright object passing over the well-appointed office.

"Tim would love that!" she whispered, as she reached for her phone to take a picture. There was a photo on the screensaver. It showed a poor, sickly seven-year-old with large haunting eyes.

As she took the photo, Bobbi felt a warm and unaccustomed glow as she looked at the light. It was so beautiful and remote and yet it seemed to speak to her of something warm and caressing. She raised the phone to take another picture when something caught her eye and immediately she let out a cry of alarm.

Four men were surrounding a lone figure below. He was tall but young, she guessed somewhere in his late teens. One of the men surrounding him leaned forward and shoved him in the chest. He staggered back towards the icy waters of the River Thames. Bobbi banged on the window of the penthouse office, shouting at the assailants to stop. It took her a second to realise she could not be heard through the thick double glazing. Immediately, she put down the phone, rushed out of the office, and ran straight to the lift. But by the time she exited the building and stood in the forecourt, readying herself for an encounter with the youths, there was no one there. She looked up and down the street.

No one.

Feeling a sudden tightness in her chest and knowing that something was wrong, she ran across the empty road, directly to the spot where she had seen the young man being attacked, her heart thumping in her chest.

A small rectangle of brightly coloured cloth lay crumpled on the ground. Bobbi approached the edge and looked over into the flowing waters; and what she saw made her cry out in horror.

6

Bobbi Cratchit shielded her eyes from the sun and made out the head of the young man, his arms flailing as he struggled in the water, disappearing and reappearing as the waves covered him. And Bobbi knew that if she did not act immediately, the man would drown. She looked around for help up and down the quayside but it was deserted. Her heart beat more rapidly in her chest as she cursed the fact that she had left her phone upstairs. She saw a flight of stone steps to her right that she knew led down to the water's edge. She ran over, calling out to the young man at the top of her voice: "Hold on!" But the words were snatched from her mouth and blown away by the wind as the young man disappeared from view again.

Panic now possessed Bobbi as she reached the steps and clambered down them. Her legs were trembling and she half-tripped on a lower step that was covered in foul-smelling green algae. Her eyes were by now streaming tears caused by the sudden blasts of arctic wind. She could smell the dark, choppy waters of the Thames. That unique dirty aroma of tides, rotting wood, and flotsam and jetsam. She could feel her hair being blown back into her face as the wind whipped up and attacked her. Sense her whole body quivering with shock and the cold and the fear that she was too late.

At the bottom of the steps was a life buoy attached to a steel bracket. Without thinking, Bobbi reached up but struggled to lift the buoy, which was larger and heavier than she imagined. She almost slipped on the green moss as she heaved the buoy away from the wall with both hands. Steadying herself and trying yet again to get her balance on the slippery surface, she threw the buoy in the direction of the floundering youth, whose dark head had re-emerged briefly in the green, turbulent waters. The adrenalin-fuelled throw took the buoy some ten feet away from the quayside steps and some five feet from the drowning figure.

"Get it!" she screamed at the top of her voice. "Hold it!"

Waves of icy cold water slopped around Bobbi's feet, making her gasp. A tugboat had passed downstream on the other side of the river, and the waves from it had reached the youth, slamming him into the buoy. He disappeared beneath the wave, the buoy covering the spot where he had been. Bobbi felt a chill run up her spine as the hand of fear gripped her heart. "Hold it!" she screamed, but he was nowhere to be seen. And that is when she saw the shard of light again. It appeared to move directly above her. She stared, mesmerised by the light. It seemed all the panic was suddenly put on hold. And out of the silence she heard a voice, somewhere far off, say: *Do it now!*

Stepping as far forward as she could and balancing uncertainly on the algae-covered step, she gathered the yellow nylon cord that was attached to the buoy and pulled. The dark head of the youth appeared again. She could plainly see his two eyes this time. They were wide with terror. She fixed on them and willed with all her might that he would hold on.

Another wave from the tug picked up the youth and flung him towards her.

"Hold on!" she screamed and this time he did, clasping the buoy with both hands. Bobbi braced herself and, with every tissue in her body, hauled on the nylon line. There was a moment when the buoy lurched away on a dipping wave, taking the young man back out towards the middle of the river. And then the buoy turned and came bobbing towards her. Bobbi adjusted the rope and gave two more mighty tugs, letting out cries as she squatted till the waters of the River Thames were up to her knees.

She could see the young man's eyes clearly now and their colour, blue as the cold sky above. Another mighty pull coincided with a last incoming wave from the tug. The buoy came suddenly crashing towards Bobbi, the rough canvas of its surface slamming into her shins, nearly knocking her off her feet. She reached down and grabbed the two outstretched hands of the young man and as she did so she noticed ugly scars on his wrists and puncture marks on his arms. His eyes locked on hers. The blue burning with the intensity of someone struggling to stay alive. Bobbi braced herself again and heaved with all her might. The young man was heavy with the weight of all his sodden clothes. But as another wave came pounding in, Bobbi slipped on the step. Both the young man's hands detached from hers and he disappeared back into the freezing waters.

7

Bobbi Cratchit may have looked weak and downtrodden but deep inside was a part as hard as a diamond. Perhaps that came from being a mother to her sickly child. Perhaps she saw a look in the eyes of the drowning man that she had seen in the eyes of her son Tim, when he was on the very edge of dying. Bobbi knew somewhere deep inside her that she could not allow this man to die, this child of another woman. She stepped down into the freezing water till it covered her thighs and grabbed the outstretched hand of the drowning man, and this time she did not let go.

She felt his bony, hard body against hers and heaved him up and out of the water with a final high-pitched scream, her knees buckling and scraping the hard stone. And as they emerged from the choppy waters, she saw blood from the scrapes where she had fallen. But if there was any pain, she did not feel it; the adrenalin saw to that.

Finally, they slipped and slid up to the top step. The young man collapsed onto his knees as they reached flat ground, but Bobbi was having none of it. Something told her that they must get out of the Arctic cold. Grabbing his arm, she began steering him towards the entrance of her office building. They staggered across the road, Bobbi barely able to support his weight. She began desperately looking around for someone to help her get him into the office when suddenly he let go of her arm and broke away, emitting a howl of pain. Heading back towards the river that had nearly swallowed him.

8

Bobbi Cratchit turned and watched, her stomach flipping at the extreme anguish in his voice. "O medalhão!" he cried out, both hands, ice blue from the cold, on the exposed skin of his chest as if ripping open the shirt under his sodden poncho.

"O medalhão – onde está meu medalhão!" he cried again, beating his chest, tears spilling down his cheeks. "O medalhão!"

He had nearly reached the river and looked as if he was searching for something, his tormented words echoing off the stone and glass canyons of the offices. Bobbi felt her own frazzled mind begin to lose what little control she still had left.

"What are you doing?" she screamed as she caught up with him.

"What is it?" The anguish of her voice must have cut through.

"O medalhão!" he said. The pity in his voice forced Bobbi to sink to her knees in front of him. And holding his trembling, young face in her hands, she looked him directly in the eye.

"You've lost something, yes?" she said. He nodded. "But we can't stay out here – we'll die of the cold!"

He took a breath and when she saw he was less panicked, took both his hands in hers. "We'll come back here and look for it, I promise!" she said as she helped him stand and turned back towards the office. She was expecting resistance but he came as meekly as a lamb, while all the time glancing back. He stumbled along as she supported him across the road and into a building with a large, impressive sign that announced: Scrooge Towers.

9

The reception area was empty and Bobbi steered the youth across the vast expanse of the cold, white marble floor. Their feet squelched as they trod, leaving pools of water at each footfall. "Sit!" Bobbi said, guiding him to a marble seat that ran adjacent to the empty reception desk. He sat down, pools of water gathering around his feet. She knelt in front of him.

"I'm Bobbi!" she said, slowly exaggeratedly, while pointing a finger at her chest, as if she was speaking to a child. "Your name?" she asked, pointing the same finger at him.

His blue eyes held her as she saw comprehension dawn.

"Jesu," he said, his voice thin and hoarse. He was not yet a man but not a boy either. A youth with a face of a man, she noticed, someone, moreover, who had aged prematurely. Then there were the marks on his wrists and arms that spoke of something ominous.

"Jesu?" she repeated. He nodded, his long dark hair dripping water onto the collar of his shirt. Bobbi held his hand as she took another breath. She felt suddenly maternal, protective. "Jesu, I'm going upstairs to call for an ambulance. YOU WAIT HERE!" She pronounced the last three words loudly and with slow deliberation. But even as she spoke, something warned her, something she could not quite lay her finger on, that he would not be there when she came back. Jesu nodded, sending small droplets of water onto Bobbi's outstretched hands.

"Good," she said, as she attempted to stand. But she was forced to stop halfway up as her legs went into spasm. Jesu reached out a hand to help her up.

"Thank you," she said, straightening stiffly. His hand was rough to her touch, like that of a labourer. And she felt a tremor run through his firm grip. A tremor of strength or was it fear? Whatever it was, Bobbi let go of his hand and stood uncertainly on her feet. The ordeal of dragging this young man out of the River Thames had finally taken its toll. She felt like collapsing on the floor, going to sleep, and never getting up. Black dots danced before her eyes. *I'm going to faint*, she thought. Instead, she held onto the edge of the reception desk and, taking deep breaths, mastered herself. Then, with a great effort of will, she held up two fingers in front of Jesu's face.

"Two minutes and I'll be back." She looked into his eyes, seeking his understanding. He nodded and the very faintest outline of a smile touched his stricken face. Bobbi let out a sigh of relief and turning, hobbled painfully across to the lift. As she walked, the true reality of what had just happened began to hit her This fragile young person, whom she knew had no malice in him, could have died right there and then in the Thames on Christmas Eve. Right in front of her eyes. She reached the lift and stepped in, taking a final look at the pathetic, sodden figure as the lift door closed over. She needed to get her phone and call the police and an ambulance. She did not know exactly why, but the irrational fear that he would be gone when she returned still haunted her. She beat down the feeling. *I'll only be a minute,* she told herself. There was a ping as the lift reached the top floor and she hurried out.

10

After Bobbi Cratchit left, Jesu looked at the lift doors for a long moment. His fingers remained at the exposed part of his neck, pawing nervously where the silver locket had been. Something tugged his eyes back to the entrance and the wall-to-ceiling glass. These gave an uninterrupted view of the deserted quayside outside and the River Thames beyond. The sun had reached its zenith, which, coming just four days after the winter solstice, was low in the sky, so low it shone directly into his eyes. He shielded them with his hand and scanned the sky but could not find the small pinprick of light. And as he sat in the quiet of the large reception area regaining his breath, he felt his whole body begin to shake violently, as he, too, finally digested what had just happened. The violence that could so easily have ended his short life and for what? Because he was a foreigner? Because he didn't speak English?

The panic he was feeling intensified as his body recalled the struggle to stay alive in the icy water. Waters that covered his mouth and nose, forcing him to gasp for air, for life. And although he was a good swimmer, the weight of his heavy, waterlogged poncho had dragged him down to what he was sure would have been his death. And as Jesu sat there, he felt again that moment that he ran out of strength and began to sink. And it was at that exact moment, as the waters covered his face, his mouth, his nose, that he remembered with stunning clarity, that same shard of bright light had reappeared. And in that moment, as he looked again at the silver shard, Jesu knew with a terrifying clarity, a clarity he had never felt so powerfully before, that he must stay alive. Feverishly, he scanned the skyline as his young eyes sought out the shard of light again. And there it was, caught between two huge office blocks on the far side of the river.

As Jesu sat there, he let out a loud sob. The sob turned into a muffled cry like that of a wounded animal. Tears welled in his eyes and spilled down his face. He was alive again when he had been lost. He was alive and could continue his quest – but even as he thought this, a sudden shadow blotted out the light. Jesu narrowed his eyes and saw that a long limousine had drawn up outside the office, out of which emerged the silhouette of a man. The figure approached the entrance of the office, obliterating the star light completely. Jesu stiffened as he felt his heart suddenly pounding in his chest. Something bad was about to happen, of that he was sure.

11

Ebenezer Scrooge was an easily outraged man. Any call on his attention, time, or especially his generosity, led to paroxysms of uncontrollable outrage. But what confronted him on entering the head office of his large financial empire left him literally lost for words.

He stood stock still, blinking hard, wondering if his eyes were playing tricks on him, for what he saw did not make sense. This was the same atrium where he had welcomed some of the world's wealthiest and most influential men: investment bankers, tech billionaires, finance ministers, and even the occasional Head of State. And yet here was something that looked like a wet, sodden, dishevelled rat sitting in a pool of water that was stretching towards his own well-heeled feet.

Scrooge blinked hard again and tried to form words. But his twitching lips refused to utter any. His fists flexed in the fine black calf leather gloves. Finally, he mastered his outrage enough to say, in a strange, high-pitched voice, "What are you doing here?"

But the young man that Scrooge was looking at did not immediately respond to his demand. Instead, Scrooge had the sense that the two intense, blue eyes were rather searching him. "I said, what are you doing here?" he repeated. His words were so loud they echoed in the hollowed confines.

The eyes of the young man kept their laser focus on Scrooge.

"Desculpe, não entendo inglês mas eu conheço você?" he said. Scrooge had a smattering of several languages from his time in international business, including Portuguese, and he thought this person had just asked if he 'knew him'.

"Of course I don't know you! You'll have to leave, I'm afraid – you can't stay here," Scrooge said, using his hand to gesture to the young man to remove himself outside. But the man did not obey and instead continued to stare back at Scrooge, while his cracked lips mouthed the words, "Mas eu conheço você?"

"No, I don't know you. Now, get out!" Scrooge said. He could see something reflected in the bloodshot eyes of the young man. It was a pinprick of light, crystal clear, dazzling, arresting. And as Scrooge concentrated on the light, he felt a shudder run through his body. The light triggered a strange, unfamiliar sensation, like a memory of someone... something. But as suddenly as the light came, it went and Scrooge's outrage returned. "I said get out!"

Again, the young man shook his head. "Não entendo inglês."

Scrooge approached the drenched figure until he was towering over him. "Are you leaving or shall I call the police – a polícia!" he shouted, fixing the young man with his stare, expecting him to flinch, as all others did. But the bedraggled figure continued to look up at him with eyes that did not display any fear. Instead, they were filled with something else. A searching, a knowing. And Scrooge began to feel the blood pound in his temples. The very idea that this man could ask if he knew him and look him in the eye in such an intimate way, as if they were somehow equals was suddenly insufferable.

"Out, out, OUT!" Scrooge shrieked again. The young man stared back as Scrooge gestured violently for him to leave.

Jesu took a deep breath and, rising shakily, began trudging towards the exit, his boots squelching with each step, leaving a wet imprint on the white marble floor.

"No! No! No!" Scrooge screamed as he strode past Jesu and back to where he had been sitting. There, a sorry-looking leather cowboy hat sat on its own. Picking it up with the thumb and forefinger of his gloved hand, Scrooge carried it back and threw it towards the man who was now standing at the open entrance. A gust of wind picked the hat up and carried it past him, where it landed on the icy road.

Jesu looked back at Scrooge as he bent to pick up his hat. He placed it on his bedraggled, wet curls of hair and continued to fix Scrooge with a questioning look. Then his mouth opened.

"Say Bobbi thank you." And with that, he turned and shuffled away.

Ebenezer Scrooge continued to stare after the retreating figure, his cruel, thin lips repeating the word, "Bobbi? Bobbi?"

He watched as the bedraggled figure turned the corner and disappeared from sight. Scrooge stayed stock-still for a full minute. There was the *ping* of the lift doors opening and he snapped around, glaring as Bobbi Cratchit appeared and stood looking around the empty atrium.

12

"Did you bring that homeless man into my building, Cratchit?" But further words died on his lips as he took in the state of his PA. The wet hair plastered over her face, clothes that were wet and muddied, and the bloodied cuts on her knees and shins.

"Did you see a young man sitting here?" Bobbi said, as she rushed over towards Scrooge.

"I'm asking you a question, Ms Cratchit. Did you bring a beggar into my building?"

"He wasn't a beggar, sir," she said, her eyes scanning the area where she had left him. "He'd been beaten up and thrown in the river. He almost drowned." She rushed past Scrooge and into the street.

"Cratchit!" Scrooge's voice boomed but Bobbi ignored him, her eyes desperately searching for Jesu. Then, with shake of her head, she turned and finally looked Scrooge in the eye. But there was not her usual fear, instead something else, something Scrooge did not recognise.

But before she could speak, blue flashing lights appeared outside the building and the ear-piercing wail of a siren brought all conversation to a halt. An ambulance roared up and braked to a halt and an ambulance man and woman clambered out. They were making for the entrance when Scrooge strode out to meet them. "Yes?" he said.

"Got a call for a man in the river—"

"That was me," said Cratchit, stepping forward. "He was pushed in by four men."

"No. No!" said Scrooge, standing between her and the ambulance officers. "As you can see, there is no one here who needs your help."

"But he was here – just a minute ago," Bobbi said as she looked at the two officers. They looked back at her, then around the empty atrium and finally back to Scrooge.

"Sorry," said the ambulanceman testily. "What's going on?"

"There was a young man but he's left," Scrooge said. "I'm sorry for the trouble you've been put to."

"Left?" Bobbi said.

Scrooge walked past Cratchit as if she was not there and began escorting the two officers outside to their ambulance. But the female officer held back.

"He got out of the water, you say?" she said to Bobbi.

"Yes, I helped him."

"Where is he now?"

Bobbi shook her head. "Don't know. He was sitting here a few moments ago."

"But he left," said Scrooge, shooting Cratchit a look that would have cut glass.

The female officer looked first at Scrooge and then at Cratchit.

"Okay, we'll have a look around." The two officers hurried over to the quayside as Scrooge turned on Cratchit.

"I'll talk to you upstairs after you've cleaned up that mess," he said, pointing to the place where Jesu had sat. "And clean yourself up," he added, his cold eyes looking her up and down.

"Where did he go?" Bobbi asked, choking back tears, but Scrooge ignored her and strode off to the lift. Cratchit turned and hurried after the ambulance crew, catching up with them at the steps down to the river. The man was coiling up the rope of the buoy that was floating half-on and half-off the bottom step.

"You used this?" he asked.

"Yes," said Bobbi.

"You should have replaced it, ma'am."

The ambulance woman placed a reassuring hand on Bobbi's shoulder. "Don't worry, we'll have a look for him." She looked down at Bobbi's bleeding knees. "Do you want us to look at those cuts – they look nasty?"

"No, it's okay," said Bobbi. "Will you call me if you see him?" She gave the ambulance woman a description and her number and was returning to the building when the ambulance man called her back.

"This yours?" He held up a silver locket. It glinted as a shaft of sunlight caught it.

"No, but I think it's his!" Bobbi said.

"You keep it safe for him, luv," the woman said as she passed it from her companion to Bobbi.

"I will," she said, holding it up and looking at it closely. Was this the object he had gone back for? She hobbled stiffly back to the entrance of her office, the silver locket clasped in her hand. And as she held it tight, it suddenly sprung open, revealing the small photo inside. She examined it, a picture of two young lovers. Something about them touched her heart, for Bobbi had once known such love. She examined the couple again, looking for any resemblance to Jesu and yes! Though the faces were faded with age, there was a ghost of his likeness in the pretty young woman. But the man? She brought the locket up close. His face was turned towards the young woman and he had inclined his head so that it touched hers. Bobbi felt a lump in her throat at the visible power of their love. The man's face was slightly turned away and it was impossible for Bobbi to find anything that reminded her of the young man she had fished out of the River Thames. Her eyes took in the faded writing on the opposing circle of the locket:

Nosso amor durará para sempre

Our love will last forever? she guessed, relying on her pigeon Portuguese.

She stood looking at the photo until she felt something soft on her face. She looked up as another spot of coldness caressed her cheek. Tiny snowflakes were trailing down towards her. Bobbi wrapped her wet cardigan tight around her chest and clasping the locket tight in her hand, she re-entered the building.

13

Scrooge stood at the window of his large, luxurious penthouse office, looking out across London's docklands. He felt a tightness, like a steel band, around his head. The Cratchit woman's behaviour filled him with an ice-cold fury. How could she possibly have thought it acceptable to bring a down-and-out into his office? He stood looking out, the leather soles of his Prada shoe tapping out a staccato rhythm on the polished mahogany floor.

His cold, pitiless eyes darted across the horizon as thoughts of punishment and retribution filled his mind. Finally, his eye settled on a solitary figure directly below him, standing on the pavement looking at something in her hand.

Scrooge's eyes narrowed; it was the Cratchit woman! Why wasn't she cleaning up the mess as he had instructed her to do? He would have words with her about that as well. He examined the small figure far below. Just an insignificant dark speck in the whiteness. How pitiful she was, he thought. A single mother with a sick, dependent child and no one to look after her. What had happened to that waster husband of hers? Run off with another woman? Scrooge couldn't remember and cared even less. She was on her own alright, so why could she not look after herself rather than waste her time on hopeless cases like the vagrant? But that was her style: pitiful, helpless.

Scrooge left the window and took his seat behind the imposing desk. He switched on the two large screens that were soon showing graphs and columns of descending and ascending figures. Asia was doing well, he thought, squinting as he examined the screen. A quick flick of his finger and a whole new set of numbers appeared. He made some inner calculations. He had been eyeing a deal for a couple of days now, waiting for the price to bottom out and it had, just as he had predicted. The price flashing in real time was perfect but only if he struck now, for there was too much volatility in their particular segment of the crypto world.

Scrooge checked that the requisite amount was in his working account and was about to press SEND when a knock on the door interrupted him.

"Not now, Cratchit," he said. There was another knock.

"Not now!" Scrooge seethed. But before he could press SEND, the unthinkable happened and someone opened the door and walked into his office unannounced.

"Cratchit, I told you—" But instead of Cratchit, a man with a young-looking face, his cheeks still rosy from the cold, strode across the room with an outstretched hand.

"Merry Christmas, Uncle!"

Scrooge's jaw muscles flexed. "Who let you in?" he said, ignoring the outstretched hand and glaring at the young man, who, on seeing no response, let it drop by his side.

"The excellent Bobbi Cratchit let me in, Uncle," he said jovially, eyeing the sofa. "Mind if I sit down?"

Before Scrooge could say "no", the man sat down and beamed a smile across at his uncle. And despite his extreme annoyance, Scrooge was still taken aback by the remarkable resemblance to his dead sister Fan. The same kind disposition and jovial approach to life. Scrooge inwardly shuddered and determined to get rid of his nephew as quickly as possible. Not just so he could close his deal, but because such misplaced optimism always got on his nerves.

Scrooge glanced back at his screen and swore under his breath. In the time Fred had been there, the graph had changed and not for the better. He removed the cursor that was hovering over the BUY button.

"Uncle, are you okay?" Fred asked. "You look a little stressed."

Scrooge shot him back a dark look.

"Your intrusion has just cost me money."

Fred fixed a look of hurt on his face. "I'm sorry, Uncle, I didn't imagine you would be working on Christmas Eve!"

Scrooge forced his face into a half smile.

"Trying to work, Fred."

"But, Uncle, why work? I read recently somewhere that you're one of the richest men in the world."

Scrooge glowered at his nephew, finding everything that met his eye repugnant. Fred had a goatee that gave his young face an arty expression. This was complemented by the tweed jacket, paisley tie, and well-worn chinos. Scuffed leather brogues in need of a polish completed the outfit. Everything Fred wore, and the way he lounged back on the sofa, indicated a man comfortable in his own skin, which, for some reason, annoyed his uncle even more. Fred's eyes continued to sparkle with just a hint of mischievous humour. "Well, aren't you one of the richest men in the world, Uncle?"

Scrooge's eyes narrowed. "You believe what you read in the media?" he spat.

Fred's eyes narrowed. "You haven't answered my question, Uncle."

Scrooge felt a flush of heat under his perfectly tailored collar. He really had to get rid of this supercilious young man.

"What do you want, Fred?"

"Uncle, you know what I want."

"I've no idea. Please enlighten me."

"Uncle, I have been visiting you every Christmas Eve with the same request for the past ten years. Come to dinner with us this Christmas Day. Celebrate with us. With my family. Your family."

Scrooge placed both hands on the desk and looked squarely at Fred.

"If you have been coming all these years, then you will not be surprised to hear the same answer. No!"

"But why not come, Uncle? I know you will spend Christmas Day all alone in that empty palace of yours. Come and join me and Mary and the kids. Come and join your family – it's the only one you have."

Scrooge took a deep breath. "Fred, I will be working."

"Working on Christmas Day, Uncle?" Fred could not hide his incredulity.

"Yes, the markets are open and there are many opportunities." Scrooge glanced back at the screen. "If you are not interrupted that is." Scrooge's eyes remained fixed on the screen and he felt a stab of pain in his chest as he calculated the growing loss caused by his nephew's arrival. And he made a mental note to punish Cratchit for letting him. No holiday for her, he thought. The look that would appear on her face when he announced the news would hardly make up for the loss but it would be better than nothing. "Anyway," Scrooge said, turning and looking at his nephew, "why this fascination with Christmas? What's it ever done for you?"

Fred laughed. "It's not about what it's just done for me, Uncle. It's about what it does for people, family, friends. All the things you don't seem to care about."

Scrooge snorted. "Christmas is a sham made up by some marketing genius to shake a few pounds out of foolish people like you. Save your money for your wife and – how many brats do you have?"

"Four and one on the way!" Fred said proudly.

"Four and one on the way…" repeated Scrooge, with unconcealed mockery. His nephew's unrelenting good humour was beginning to make him feel nauseous. "Keep what little money you have for your… brats."

Fred shook his head. "Uncle, I just want to share some precious time with you before it is too late…"

"Too late for what?" said Scrooge, laughing darkly. "I intend to outlast you all! Now if you'll excuse me, I have work to do."

Scrooge leant forward and pressed the office intercom on his desk. The disembodied voice of Bobbi Cratchit echoed in the room, "Yes, sir?"

"My nephew is leaving; please come and escort him off the premises."

There was a slight pause. "Yes, sir."

"Uncle," said Fred, pushing himself up from the sofa, "we will always extend our invitation to you."

"How touching," said Scrooge, his eyes now on the doors to his office as he waited for Cratchit.

"And in the meantime, I wish you a very happy Christmas, Uncle."

"Yes, yes, good afternoon," said Scrooge. He was aching to get back to the screen and see if he could salvage anything.

"You are precious to us, Uncle, the last remaining link to my dear mother, Fan."

At the mention of his sister's name, Scrooge felt a deeply unsettling tightness in his chest. He had to end this encounter now.

"Good afternoon, Fred," he said, his voice rising. But Fred was undeterred, the smile on his face perhaps betraying that he was getting some satisfaction from ribbing his cantankerous uncle.

"And so, on behalf of Mary and Jonathan, Debbie, Lance and Meredith," he continued, drawing out each name, "I wish you season's greetings."

"Good afternoon!" Scrooge said, almost shouting, his fists clenched.

"And a very merry and happy new year!" By now the two men were facing each other like combatants, Scrooge's face flushed red with anger and Fred's wreathed in a broad smile. What would have happened next was avoided by the appearance of Bobbi Cratchit.

"My nephew is leaving," snapped Scrooge, returning his gaze to the screen. Fred turned to Bobbi.

"And a very happy Christmas to you, Bobbi Cratchit!"

"And to you, sir," she said, her eyes darting nervously to the scowling Scrooge. But her boss was examining the screen, his face tense, his lips tight, his hands trembling as they hovered over the keyboard. "I'll show you out, sir," said Bobbi, leading the way.

"And close the door behind you—" said Scrooge, but they had gone, leaving the door wide open. He turned back to the screen, his jaw muscles flexing.

14

Jesu had scoured the area where he had last seen his silver locket after being thrown back out onto the streets. Shivering with cold, he examined the steps where he had been hauled up by Bobbi, one of the kindest and bravest women he had ever met. But he found no trace of the pendant, even though he had stood on the bottom steps ankle-deep in icy water looking for any glint of the silver casing. That was until a large wave came barrelling in and nearly swept him off his feet. The shock of that and the fear of drowning again forced him to abandon his search, and as he shuffled away, he saw an ambulance roar up to Scrooge Towers, its lights flashing. Was that the one Bobbi had summoned for him, he wondered. But as the icy winds buffeted him, he knew he must seek shelter and get out of these sodden, wet clothes if he wasn't going to freeze to death. Clothes so cold that his trouser legs were turning into stiff boards.

He turned a corner and passed a stretch of wasteland between Scrooge Towers and another towering office block and there, in the middle, he spied a workman's hut. The door was flapping ajar in the wind and it beckoned.

Jesu paused and scanned the horizon, a sudden nervous tension seizing him. Where were his assailants? Did they live nearby? Seemed unlikely. His attackers were hardly the city-slicker types, so where had they come from? Perhaps it was safer if he was out of sight? Jesu stumbled over the snow and reaching the flapping door of the hut, looked inside.

The floor of the workmen's hut was covered in snow but there appeared to be a small-ringed gas stove and the remnants of a couple of Pot Noodle plastic containers on a dirty countertop. Jesu glanced back at the quayside road just in time to see a taxi passing and he could just make out the shape of a large woman sitting in the back. With a deep sigh, Jesu wrenched close the door of the hut. Finally he was out of the bitter cold, though his breath still plumed the air. He would try to get the stove to work but first he must rest. There was a pile of discarded carpets and rubber mats piled up on one side of the hut which Jesu, feeling a bout of dizziness, flung himself on, and soon he was out to the world and dreaming fitfully.

And in that dream, he was visited by the tall, vicious man who glowered over him, threatening to expel him even from this small hovel. A man with a blank face. A man that

Jesu somehow thought he knew – all he had to do was fill in the face and make the person real, just like the man in the photo of his precious locket. But as he slept, there was a rustle in the garbage and something appeared, sniffing the air, something that posed a real danger to the man lying fast asleep on the piles of rugs.

15

Doctor Ellie Adebayo was sitting forward in her taxi seat. She was trying to tally up the amount she had collected from local businessmen for her refugee outreach programme HELP! So far, the pickings had been slim. People refused to take her call or said they were away on holidays. She was a long way short of her target and with just one potential donor left on her list. *I have to get this done!* She kept repeating it herself: *I have to get this done!* But even getting in to see people was proving a challenge. She glanced down at the list scribbled on the back of a lunch receipt by the new intern: Mr SCORPIUS & Mr EBENEZER of Scrooge Towers. Doctor Ellie frowned. It was a strange coincidence that Scrooge Towers was next to the wasteland where her charity held their annual Christmas Outreach. Surely the Scrooges would have heard about this charitable Christmas event held in their backyard? For her part she had never heard of the Scrooges and their nearby tower. But perhaps knowing that they were neighbours would loosen the purse strings of this potential benefactor?

She was glancing out of the window when a movement caught her eye; someone standing by a shed in the middle of the wasteland. Someone who looked, to her professional eye, like they were in trouble. Was it one of her regulars? Doctor Ellie whispered a prayer for them. Perhaps they'd hear the singing and dancing later and come and join them.

The taxi braked to a halt in front of the impressive entrance to Scrooge Towers and, clambering out, Doctor Ellie manoeuvred her large frame up the short flight of steps and stood before the open glass doors. There appeared to be no one inside, so she looked for an intercom to announce her arrival. She heard the sound of voices and glancing to her right, saw two people deep in conversation. One was a young man with a smiling, ruddy face and the other a woman in her thirties who looked, even from this distance, tired and drawn. Doctor Ellie tried to catch their eye but they were too deeply engrossed to take notice. She sighed and stepped into the lobby. It was empty, as was the reception desk. She moved over to the lifts unchallenged and examined the list that showed what was on each floor. The lift door was already open and, taking this as a sign, Doctor Ellie murmured "Okay," got in, and pressed the button for the top floor. The lift doors closed and transported her up to the rooftop penthouse and the office of: EBENEZER SCROOGE CEO.

16

Ebenezer Scrooge turned his attention back to his screen and cursed when he saw that the deal he was about to make when Fred arrived had vanished. He would have to make up for that loss, and quickly. He closed his eyes and concentrated. There was something at the back of his mind. Some deal… Ah yes, he thought, as he took his cursor and scanned the Shanghai markets. He had received a tip from a "friend" the week before. The "friend" was in the China stock markets official governance body and had owed Scrooge a favour. It was something that was not strictly legal, but who would know? Scrooge smiled thinly as he located the small investment company that was trading what looked like a ridiculously high-risk Chinese crypto coin.

Scrooge clicked on the trades and examined the graph. His eyes narrowed as he focused on the last three days. If he had not received the insider information, he would not have touched this transaction with a bargepole. But if what his "friend" had said was true, he would make enough to cover the missed opportunity his nephew's arrival had cost him and more to spare. But he'd need to be quick, for as he checked the trading terms, he realised that the market was closing for the Christmas break in exactly four minutes. His well-manicured fingers splayed wide and started drumming a staccato rhythm on the mahogany desk as he began calculating his bid. It could not be too large – that could alert the authorities and possibly trigger a suspension of his account. No, it had to be just right. The drumming continued, a sign that he was poised to strike. The graph was climbing as final bids flooded in before the close for the Christmas break. The tip of Scrooge's tongue came out, like a serpent's, and licked his bloodless lips. The smile broadened and he lowered his finger to complete the sale when a loud knock on the open door of his office forced him to look up.

The sight that greeted Scrooge did not please him. Standing framed by the doorway stood a large black woman. Her dark skin was offset by the kaleidoscope of bright colours of the shawl thrown around her shoulders. Her jet-black, frizzy hair was bejewelled by the last vestiges of snowflakes yet to melt. Scrooge's mouth hung open involuntarily as he looked at this formidable-looking woman who had somehow breached his wall of security and made her way into his inner sanctum unannounced. The woman's bright eyes challenged him, as she said cheerily, "Are you Scorpius or Ebenezer Scrooge?"

The mention of his father's name – a name that had never been uttered before in this building – caught Scrooge entirely off guard. Suddenly, the name Scorpius was accompanied by a face. A face that Scrooge had all but obliterated from his memory. He shuddered inwardly and looked angrily at the woman. "I'm Ebenezer Scrooge. My father, Scorpius, has been dead for many years." And Scrooge felt the tightness in his chest return, as he suddenly realised a terrible coincidence. "He died on this very night, twenty years ago."

"Well," said the woman, rescuing Scrooge from the unpleasant recollection, "I'm sure you will be just as generous as he was."

The word "generous" brought Scrooge crashing back to his senses.

"Generous?" he said, his voice sharp, his whole body on edge.

"Yes," said the large woman, entering the room and approaching his desk. "I'm sure you and your late father would be happy to support our refugee charity."

It was not often that Ebenezer Scrooge was lost for words but this was just such an occasion. The sheer unexpectedness of the intrusion and the mention of his father's name combined with the word "generous" left Scrooge in a state of shock. If the woman had any sense of

Scrooge's confusion, she did not show it. Instead, she approached his enormous desk and, reaching out, offered her hand.

"My name is Doctor Ellie and I'm very pleased to meet you, Ebenezer!" She beamed down at him with two large brown eyes. Scrooge shook his head severely.

"I'm sorry but a meeting with me is impossible." He glanced at the screen and saw that he had just over three minutes before the markets closed. "You'll have to leave." But Doctor Ellie only laughed out loud.

"What do you mean leave, Ebenezer? I've only just arrived!"

Scrooge felt a tightness in his throat. "You can't just barge your way into my office like this, Doctor – whatever your name is – without an appointment. You'll have to leave."

"Mr Ebenezer," she said, with a hearty chuckle. "There was no one to barge past when I came into your building. And," she emphasised the word by glancing back over her shoulder, "your door was wide open. Not much barging there!" she said, breaking into a hearty laugh.

Scrooge was not used to people disagreeing with him. He felt a rising anger burn his throat, an anger that burnt the stronger as he glanced at the screen. He had just over two minutes to make his deal. Again, his thoughts were interrupted by the woman's booming, enthusiastic voice.

"What I have to say will only take a minute." She raised a finger and wagged it in Scrooge's face. "And really, you shouldn't get so stressed, Ebenezer – you'll raise your blood pressure." She held his stare and spoke in a comforting doctor's bedside manner. "Remember, I'm a physician; have you had your blood pressure checked recently?"

Scrooge was about to scream at her to get out but something stopped him. Perhaps it was the intuition that this was not another Bobbi Cratchit who would quiver and quail at his words. He took another glance at the screen. Ninety seconds left.

"You have one minute exactly!" He held up his wrist so they could both see his elegant and very expensive watch.

"Why thank you, Ebenezer," she said, lowering her considerable weight into the leather chair that creaked in complaint. Scrooge felt the burning tightness spread to his throat as he realised that this encounter would certainly take longer than a minute. Should he buy? Something told him not to be too hasty. He kept his finger poised over the BUY button, left one eye on the clock while shifting the other to the large and intensely annoying woman that had gate-crashed his office. Where had Cratchit been?

"Mr Scrooge," Doctor Ellie said, settling herself into the creaking chair while adjusting her shawl. "I work with people who are adrift in life as they were in the boats that brought them here. That is" – she spread her hands wide – "the few that survived that horrendous journey."

Scrooge watched the clock ticking down on his computer screen, his impatience bubbling underneath as Doctor Ellie continued. "Many of these refugees end up here with nothing but the clothes on their backs and it is my job." Doctor Ellie shook her head sagely. "Indeed, it is my privilege to help these people find shelter, food, clothing, and some comfort, particularly at this cold, unforgiving time of year."

Scrooge blinked hard: "Are there no government schemes to help these… people?"

"Ah yes, Mr Scrooge," Doctor Ellie replied, "but they are all overwhelmed at this time of the year. Honestly, they just can't cope."

"No holding centres to receive and process such…" he searched for the word, "unfortunates?"

The smile on Doctor Ellie's face beginning to fade. "Oh yes, Mr Scrooge, many holding centres to process these 'unfortunates' as you call them. But they are all at capacity."

Scrooge glanced at the clock. The minute was up and so was his patience. "I'm sorry, but I pay my taxes – and lots of them – to support these schemes. I cannot help you."

"It's not ME you're helping, Mr Scrooge," she said, the smile entirely disappearing from her face. "It's the less well-off. Souls that have nowhere to go. No one to help. I am talking about mothers and children and babies. People who actually live on the wasteland at the back of this very office. Surely you can help them, Mr Scrooge?"

Scrooge felt the burning sensation reach all the way up till it filled his throat. He glanced at the screen. Barely thirty seconds to make his deal.

"I have seen these people. They are trespassing and have no right to be there."

Doctor Ellie's eyes widened. "And what will happen to them in this cold weather, Mr Scrooge? Unless we help them. Unless *you* help them, they will surely die."

Scrooge felt the accusatory stare bore right through him. And in that moment, he snapped. "Let them die! It will stop them from cluttering up our streets – cluttering up my reception!" The image of the young man – more rat than human – filled his seething mind.

"What?" Doctor Ellie said, stunned. "Reception? What are you talking about?"

"I will not give you one penny. Is that clear?"

Scrooge was now also leaning across his desk, his face flushed red, his neck muscles straining.

Doctor Ellie held his stare for a long moment. Finally, she shook her head as her smile returned. "It's very clear, Mr Scrooge," she said, placing both her hands on the tubular steel arms of her chair and pushing herself upright. Her large, imposing body suddenly dwarfed his.

"You've got everything, haven't you, Mr Scrooge," she said, glancing around the plush room as she readjusted her scarf. "Everything but a heart." There was a pause as her eyes studied his. "And you know what… I pity you, Mr Scrooge. I really do." And with a final, piteous look at Scrooge, she turned and left.

Scrooge followed her with his eyes, which then flicked back to the screen. The clock had just gone red and the market had closed. He swore an oath and slumped back in his chair. Cratchit would pay dearly for this he seethed, as he reached over and hit the intercom button.

17

Bobbi Cratchit held the silver locket in her hand and looked at her phone for perhaps the hundredth time that afternoon. No call from the ambulance crew. A feeling of despair had begun to fill her whole body. Questions tormented her mind, relentless, unanswered, and the image of the young man's face seemed imprinted on her soul. Images of him looking at her with those blue eyes as he reached out to her from the seething waters of the River Thames.

Then the desperation that he had felt on realising he had lost his silver locket, the very one she held in her hand.

Bobbi moved uncomfortably in her chair at the thought. Or, more accurately, she tried to move, for her whole body went into a spasm. Her neck was stiff. Her arms felt like they had been torn out of their sockets. And as for her knees? They were swollen and bloodied. It was painful to even stand.

After she had returned to the office building, she had cleaned herself up as best she could but she had no spare tights. And as all the nearby shops were closed, she had finally thrown the ruined pair in the bin and had gone barelegged. She was painfully aware of her exposed knees, bruised and covered in drying, bloody scabs. She sighed and looked out of her window and down to the quayside where the young man had been. But all she saw was a snowy white landscape bisected by the black river. She could clearly make out the steps down which she had gone to rescue him. The step from which she had emerged minutes later, exhausted yet elated with the bedraggled, coughing Jesu.

She blinked away tears at the memory. Had it actually happened? Had she saved that strange young man or was it all a dream? If it had not been for the silver locket clenched in her hand and the bloodied scrapes on her knees, she would have doubted her sanity.

Bobbi stood up and hobbled stiffly over to the window. And here she stood, resting her troubled brow against the cool glass for relief, her eyes searching endlessly, hopelessly. But all that greeted her were the curtains of snow that were covering the streets below in a white blanket. A blanket that was virgin, save for the black tyre tracks left by a skidding vehicle.

Her eyes scanned the pavements but there were no footprints. She blinked and focused on the far side of the river, trying to find any signs of Jesu in the great canyons that were formed between the towering office blocks. But all she could see was the occasional taxi slip-sliding its way along the icy streets and a large yellow city of London snow truck, with flashing lights that twinkled orange and red as it gritted the road. She looked up at the lowering clouds that covered London and she saw again, in her mind's eye the scars on Jesu's wrists and arms. Had he once tried to commit suicide? It would seem so, and was he a heroin user? She felt a heaviness in her stomach and stab of pain in her chest as she saw again his young, blue imploring eyes.

"Is he okay?" she asked the sky, with the intensity of a prayer. And at that moment, she thought she saw the shard of light between a rent in the clouds. And her heart suddenly leapt with an unaccustomed joy. But the clouds closed over and the light was lost. The buzzer on her intercom snapped her from her reverie. It was Scrooge calling her. Scrooge… the man who had sent the shivering Jesu back out into the storm to face an uncertain fate.

Bobbi took one last, fruitless look out at London before turning slowly and painfully to meet the man who held her fate in his hands.

18

Down on the docks, a thin blanket of snow was beginning to settle. Strong gusts of wind sent eddies of snow forward and back, rising and falling like mini-tornados, before depositing large mounds of snow in the doorways and windows of the tall buildings that looked out onto the Thames. The empty streets had an eerie silence as the snow gathered into one great white sheet. And as the blanket settled, there came a stillness. It was as if the blanket of snow was quieting all forms of life. No birds flew. Even the raucous seagulls seemed to be taking a rest. A strange energy had descended around the buildings owned by Ebenezer Scrooge. Something was building. Something just beyond perception. Something powerful yet invisible.

Meanwhile, the only other thing that moved was the great River Thames, like a huge, black coiled snake, weaving its way through the concrete collection of glass and steel that reached up to the sky. And as the high, invisible winds blew the clouds over London, ragged rents and occasional tears were ripped in its leaden fabric and through these narrow gaps appeared the faint shard of light. A light that seemed to glow with the energy of another world.

And as the light shone, there was a murmur, undetectable to the human ear. A murmur of faint voices, high-pitched, shrill, speaking a language unrecognisable to human kind. That was, unless the listener had a certain sense or facility: an acuteness of spirit, a gladness of heart, or the innocence of a child.

19

High above, in the penthouse, Ebenezer Scrooge was looking unusually stern as he waited for Bobbi Cratchit to arrive. The losses that he had suffered due to first his nephew's intrusion and then the black doctor's interruption stung him and would not let go. And like a fish caught on a barbed hook, Scrooge twisted and turned, restless and tormented. That profit, he kept reminding himself, would have added nicely to his daily portfolio, accounting for a small part of the amount he had to earn each and every day. Now he would have to stay later, longer, till the figure was met. For Ebenezer Scrooge was a man possessed. A man on a secret mission. It was an almost impossible mission but one that drove him on daily, by the minute and by the second, until nothing and no one else mattered. And the mission? To become the richest man in the world.

Where had this ambition come from?

It had occurred to Scrooge on a visit to Downing Street some five years previously, a visit he would never have made if it had not been a personal invite from the Prime Minister herself. And even then, Scrooge had done all he could to avoid the event, for he hated all such public gatherings. But as Scrooge sat in Number 10, bored and impatient to leave, an address by the American Secretary of State had suddenly made him sit up and take notice. The Secretary mentioned the impossibility of anyone but an American ever becoming the richest person in the world. It was said as a joke but Scrooge was the only person that did not laugh. And in that moment Scrooge decided to prove the Secretary of State wrong. And to prove himself right. For he had, up to that moment, achieved pretty much everything he had strived to achieve. The first goal was making himself self-sufficient after his acrimonious split from his father. The second was exceeding his father's fortune, which he had done within a year. And so, his fortune had grown but Scrooge knew deep inside he needed something else to spur him on and to keep him going. Consequently, this soaring ambition had been born. But the challenge Scrooge set himself was not about the money or glory but rather as a bloody-minded way to exercise his iron will. To prove to himself that he could do it. After all, he had no family. No children. No wife. No friends even. And so began his personal quest: to become the world's richest man.

Scrooge was already by that time a billionaire but he did not feature in the list of the world's top one hundred richest men and women. It took him all his skill and two years of considerable hard work to muscle in on the world's top twenty list, coming in at nineteen. He celebrated this milestone by working through the night and making close to £500 million on one deal. That made him happy. But it was still nowhere near enough. Scrooge was discovering that entering the elite pantheon of the mega-rich had its own unique challenges. To scale up his considerable fortune to match the biggest and best in the world was not as easy as even he had imagined. For there were, he was discovering, vast fortunes that had been built over decades. Fortunes whose very size allowed them to grow at exponential rates. Getting to number one involved a massive game of catch-up. But the mission had entirely possessed Ebenezer Scrooge's hungry soul, making even the small losses he had suffered that very morning unbearable.

Just three years after he entered the world's top twenty, he made tenth place on the list. A year later, he was fourth. But then things had slowed down, precipitated by a crash in the cryptocurrency market that dropped him back to sixteenth place. This had irked Scrooge beyond reckoning. But Scrooge was as hard as nails. He knew how to ride the waves of a financial storm. He made a series of extraordinary gambles that left the world of finance gasping. He waged, at one stage, his entire fortune on shorting the volatile crypto market. The market temporarily rebounded and nearly wiped him out, and financial editors around the world began writing his obituary. But Scrooge held his nerve and made one fortune as the market bottomed. Then another as the market soared. The combined fortunes catapulted Scrooge directly to number three. He was now behind a Saudi oil magnate at two and the legendary American female entrepreneur Lucila Van Der Holt at one. Der Holt owned the world's largest AI conglomerate. And it was her very own algorithms and her cutting-edge AI investment programmes that pushed her on to become the first US dollar trillionaire. But Scrooge had hatched an outrageous plan to surpass her. A plan two years in the making. And that plan would be sprung as New Year's Day dawned, now barely a week away.

Scrooge opened his secret ledger, an account protected by an elaborate blockchain, and took a few precious moments to revisit some of the micro-details of the plan, fine-tuning it with his razor-sharp mind. Then he took a moment to do what he loved most: to count the almost impossible number of zeros that made up his fortune before sitting back and imagining them swelling so they outnumbered his competitor. Had Der Holt any idea what was about to hit her? He doubted it. There would be no leak, no tip-off. For no one knew of his plan. He worked entirely alone. And he was, he admitted, ruthless and without conscience or a heart, all the necessary requisites needed to become the world's richest person.

Scrooge looked again at the current tally of his secret wealth. His eyes caressed the almost impossible number of zeros – zeros that he had accumulated with painstaking patience and a steel nerve. His face softened in the glare of the computer screen and there was an unaccustomed look in his eyes. It was the look of love. Love of the green digits glowing softly on his screen. Love of the power they gave him. Love of money.

Scrooge began calculating his day's gains. They were few, due mainly to the two interruptions caused, in part, by Cratchit's incompetence. She really would have to go if she continued in this vein. He sat watching the door as he heard her footsteps approach, crouched at his desk like a lion waiting to pounce on its kill.

20

Bobbi Cratchit stood in the doorway of Scrooge's office, feeling acutely self-conscious of her appearance. She did not want to approach Scrooge's desk for fear of what he would say. So, she stood watching as his eyes looked her up and down, taking in the bloodied knees, the ruined cardigan, the sunken eyes.

"Today your incompetence cost me a fortune. Why should I keep you on, Cratchit?" He said all this without emotion but with the very faintest trace of a smile in his cruel eyes. Bobbi felt a rising panic grip her throat.

"I'm sorry, sir, I was trying to save that young man…" Her words petered out as she realised the futility of arguing with Scrooge. And then, of course, was the matter of her debt. And even as the thought occurred in her mind, he seemed to read it, as he always did.

"Should you not think first about saving yourself, Cratchit?" he said with a soft venom. "Your debt to me is a long way from being repaid." He paused to let his words sink in. "I hope you have not forgotten the consequences of not repaying it."

Bobbi looked at Scrooge and felt the bile rise in her throat. There was only one thing she could never tolerate and that was an attack on her son, indirect or otherwise, for she had borrowed the money to fund an operation that would not have otherwise happened. "That was to save Tim's life, sir!"

Scrooge smiled back at her, always a sign of him at his most dangerous. "I paid you two year's wages in advance for this 'operation' and so far you have paid off" – he glanced at his screen – "four months minus interest. If I have to dismiss you for incompetence, which at the moment is a distinct possibility" – his eyes bored into her like a laser – "I will take every remedy to get back the money you owe me." Scrooge watched with satisfaction as the threat hit home but that was not all he had to say. "Furthermore, you will not be getting a good recommendation from me when you go searching for a new job."

Bobbi looked back at Scrooge without saying anything.

Scrooge considered her for a long moment, weighing his retribution.

"Due to your sheer incompetence, I will have to work tomorrow. I expect you to do the same. After all, that is only fair."

But Bobbi could not let this pass unchallenged. "It's Christmas Day, sir. I'm afraid I won't get anyone to mind Tim."

Scrooge held her in his pitiless stare. "That is not my concern, Cratchit. I'll see you here at the usual time."

Bobbi looked at Ebenezer Scrooge and opened her mouth to speak. That was until she saw her defeat writ large in his eyes. She felt the surge of bile in her mouth again, followed by the need to be sick. Her knees were aching with a dull pain. All she wanted was to get home to her son and curl up with him, cry and forget this day from hell. She nodded curtly.

"And don't be late," said Scrooge, joining the tips of his fingers together in a steeple. Slowly and painfully, she turned and left as Scrooge's face broke into a broad, malevolent smile.

21

When Scrooge left the office ten minutes later, the snow had finally ceased. He ignored George's greeting and settled in the back seat of his giant limo, cocooned in a luxury that few would ever experience. But Scrooge did not look happy or comfortable. Instead, he stared straight ahead of him with an intensity that the chauffeur knew meant only one thing. His master was angry. Best to steer clear.

George flicked the indicator to pull away from the pavement and waved to the disconsolate figure of Bobbi Cratchit making her way home in the snow. It was unthinkable Scrooge would give her a lift. Unthinkable that Ebenezer Scrooge would do anything charitable on this Christmas Eve, or Christmas Day, or any other day. George accelerated the huge car away, suddenly feeling a sense of relief that this was his last journey with the man who did everything to make his life, and the lives of everyone around him, a misery. George did chance one last glance back in the mirror. Scrooge did not meet his eye. Instead, with a face like thunder, he stared unblinking into the middle distance.

George resumed his driving, careful of the icy roads and did not look back again.

Scrooge had no clear idea why this small but persistent knot of anxiety continued to grow in the pit of his stomach. It was as if a storm was about to break over him. A storm that had been building all day. But a storm about what? What in God's name was happening?

Scrooge was used to controlling his feelings with an iron will. Control your feelings and you can control others was his mantra. So Scrooge was determined to get rid of this annoying sense that something bad was about to happen. He scoured his memories for people or events that could have upset him. First off was Cratchit and her contribution to his financial setbacks, but he had exacted a price from her. She would not mess up again. And if she did, it would be the last time. He thought hard again.

There was that obnoxious black doctor but he had run her empty-handed out of his office. Who else had crossed him that day? His nephew, Fred, came to mind. But he was just an idiot who no one took seriously. No, it was none of them. So, who or what exactly was bothering him? Where was the sense of growing dread coming from?

Scrooge's brow furrowed as he turned and looked out of the window. The limo was now driving along the

Embankment and Scrooge watched the last of the Christmas revellers making their way home. The car swept through Trafalgar Square and he spied the giant Christmas tree surrounded by crowds of families. Some were singing carols. Some dancing arm-in-arm. All seemed to be having a good time. Scrooge's lip curled in contempt. *What gullible fools*, he thought, *all taken in by the humbug.*

The limo turned up the Mall and Buckingham Palace emerged into view. It was truly a winter wonderland all decked in white but Scrooge had no time for any of that. Instead, his mind continued to sift through the detritus of his day as he sought out the source of his growing unease. It was as they were passing Victoria Station the epiphany occurred and an image exploded into Scrooge's consciousness.

It was the naming of his dead father Scorpius! Finally, he had tracked it down. A grim smile played on Ebenezer Scrooge's thin lips and his nostrils flared as the hatred for his father filled his soul. Scorpius… the word had not passed his lips in many long years. Scorpius. SCORPIUS! The father who had been his enemy from the very moment that he had drawn his very first breath.

But despite this epiphany, Scrooge still shifted uncomfortably in his seat. His discovery had somehow led to him feeling a deeper unease. Most times when he tracked down uncomfortable feelings, he could expel them and return to his normal existence of not feeling anything at all. Anything that is, except his love of money. But on this occasion, it was different. From the moment that awful black woman had mentioned his father's name, Scrooge had felt this deep unease, and the feeling had not gone away. In fact, it was growing by the second. Scrooge felt a pain in his head, as if someone was tightening a steel band around his skull. He felt the palms of his hands itch and, glancing down, saw that they were slippery with sweat. What was going on?

He glared at George, thinking that the chauffeur must have noticed his obvious discomfort. But the chauffeur's peaked cap was pointing directly ahead, his head rock steady and his old shoulders hunched as he gripped the steering wheel. The limo hit a road bump rather too hard (it had been hidden by the snow) and Scrooge felt every nerve in his body jangle as he was jolted in his seat. He wanted to scream out but why?

Scrooge placed both his hands face down on the plush leather seat, to steady himself as his thoughts turned, again without his consent, to his father Scorpius. The man had barely warranted one serious thought in the twenty years since his death, so why now? Scrooge made up his mind. There would be no more thoughts of his father.

That was it!

And suddenly he felt better. He relaxed back in his comfortable seat and directed his mind as to what he would do for the rest of the evening. First, he would make sure the chauffeur dropped him off at the church next door to his house. That way, he would not have to deal with any emotional farewells or appeals for him to give back the old Mercedes. Scrooge knew his father's wishes. Scorpius and George had a bond of friendship that Scrooge thought inappropriate. One should never get close to the servants; they would only rip you off, he believed.

So, no car for George, Scrooge thought. A smile of satisfaction played on his lips. He would avoid the old chauffeur altogether and smoke a cigar in the grounds of the church instead. Then he would go inside for a glass of fine brandy before checking the Asian markets. But even as he started planning his night ahead, the unease hit back to twist his intestines. And suddenly it became clear to him why that new feeling was assailing him.

22

Scrooge sifted through the embers of his memories. He had been in his private members club playing a game of poker. He remembered he had forgotten to turn off his phone and nearly didn't take the call when it came in, and that was his first mistake.

"Eb." Fan's voice was high-pitched, tearful. "He's asking for you. You must come. He won't last the night."

"Who won't last the night," Scrooge had said, genuinely perplexed as to who she was referring to.

"Your father, Ebenezer!" she shot back. "He's in St Thomas's, you must come!"

There is always that moment. A time of decision, when fate can go one way or another. This phone call was just such a moment for Ebenezer Scrooge. He remembered looking at his playing partners who were eyeing him disapprovingly for taking a call in the middle of their game and made up his mind. He hated the old man and it would be hypocritical to do anything else.

"I'm sorry, Fan," he said with barely a pause. "You can tell him I won't be coming. I'm sure he'll understand." (Even now, as he recalled it, Scrooge felt a slight pang of remorse at the last remark.)

"For God's sake, Ebenezer, he's your—" But Scrooge had hung up and returned to his game. Winning, if he remembered rightly, £1,283 or was it €1,382? He'd have to check. It was only the next morning, when he turned his phone back on, that he received a text from his sister.

Your father died at midnight, Ebenezer. He was calling your name as he passed away. You SHOULD HAVE COME.

And Ebenezer Scrooge remembered that he had felt a brief moment of unease, knowing his father had died calling out his name. But that moment also passed and Scrooge had rarely, if ever, thought of his father again. Until this day, when a black doctor had uttered his name in his office. And that night, when he had found himself remembering Fan's call at the exact time it had been made twenty years ago to the second. And as the car sped across London, Scrooge closed his eyes tight and with a clenched jaw willed his mind to stop. For a moment, all was quiet and all he could hear was the gentle hum of the engine and the shift of the gears as George steered the great car. But just as his jaw was relaxing Scrooge heard a voice somewhere far off cry out his name: *Scrooge!*

Scrooge's body stiffened and all his senses were suddenly alert. He had not imagined the voice, he was sure of that. He felt his blood pounding in his temples as he waited, spellbound. And after a long moment it came again, louder, more distinct, as if emerging from a lost tunnel: *SCROOGE!*

He snapped open his eyes and looked around to see where the voice was coming from, panting like an animal. "Did you hear that, George?" he said.

"Hear what, sir?"

Scrooge ignored the driver and scanned the streets. On the right were well-appointed London mansions, dark save for the occasional Christmas tree blinking in the gloom. His head swivelled to the left and he saw the great River Thames twinkling with a strange luminescence, as if cascades of orange blood were leaking on its dark, troubled waters. And Scrooge's eyes were drawn up into the sky, to see from whence this strange reflection was coming. His eyes searched the far side of the river, climbing over the bridges and buildings. And suddenly Scrooge let out a cry of alarm so loud that George braked hard and momentarily lost control of the great vehicle, which went slip-sliding across the icy London road and straight at a bollard.

23

"Mr Scrooge – what is it?"

George had brought the car back under control and had braked to a halt on the Chelsea Embankment. And he watched in a kind of fascinated horror as his boss flung open the car door and, ignoring an oncoming motorcyclist, stalked across the road till he was standing alone, his hands on the granite stone wall, his face looking out over the river.

After a moment's indecision, George got out, shuffled over, and stood awkwardly by his boss's side.

"Did you see it?" Scrooge asked. His voice terse, his eyes searching for a spot in the sky over Battersea Park. George paused. Bitter experience had warned him to tread carefully when his boss was in "one of his moods". But this mood was beyond anything George had ever experienced. It was more than a mood, it felt like a kind of insanity.

"Sorry, sir, saw what?"

"It!" Scrooge stabbed at the horizon with his index finger but George could see nothing except inky blackness. After a moment's hesitation, George mumbled an apology and hobbled back to the car. Traffic was light but still he could not leave the vehicle unattended on this busy stretch of London road where drivers were apt to gun fast cars along at reckless speed. He reached the driver's door and turned to look at Scrooge, who was as still as a statue, gazing up at the sky.

A few moments later, he heard the passenger door open and Scrooge resumed his seat.

"Back home, sir?" George asked nervously, glancing in the rear-view driver's mirror. Scrooge nodded curtly and sat erect in the plush leather seats, his mind feeling as if it was fast spiralling out of control – a sensation he had rarely experienced.

"I saw it!" he whispered to himself. "I saw it." His mind replayed in vivid detail the image of a luminous ball of light that he had seen travelling in the sky alongside the car. It was as if the sun itself had come down from the sky and was travelling alongside him. And an eye had emerged from the centre of the light as he heard his name called out loud: *Scrooge! SCROOGE!*

Scrooge held the fingers of his right hand up to his forehead. "Ebenezer Scrooge, get a grip on yourself!" he hissed under his breath. He blinked hard, trying to remove the image that was burnt into his retina. But it remained stubbornly there. Gyrating, oscillating, coruscating bands of orange light. Scrooge stabbed the tips of his fingers into his forehead – *It was not there!* He kept repeating: *It was not there!*

And this was how George found Ebenezer Scrooge some ten minutes later, when he opened the passenger door. And it took the flood of cold air to alert Scrooge to the fact that they had arrived home.

Adjusting his overcoat, Ebenezer Scrooge pushed himself out of the vehicle and stood upright. A gust of ice-cold air buffeted him and he drank in a great gulp of air, as if trying to clear his chaotic mind. Instinctively, he looked up at the giant steeple of the church that towered over him. He then strode past George, making directly for the rusting iron gate that was set in the wall of his garden and gave private access to the church grounds and the graveyard beyond.

"Good eve—" George said, but the words died on his lips as he realised that his boss was entirely preoccupied. With a shake of his old head, George closed the car door and began trudging over to his small driver's lodge, located at the back of the vast house. There he would change into his day clothes, hang up his chauffeur's uniform (which did not belong to him), replace the car keys, and leave the service of the Scrooge family for good. And as he trod through the snow, he passed the Panton Mercedes Benz, now covered in a blanket of white. George stood in silence for a long moment, looking at the vehicle that should have been his but would instead rust away.

George held back a sob and continued trudging on. He had almost left the front of the house when something caught his attention and his rheumy eyes focused on the graveyard. There was the tall outline of the figure of Ebenezer Scrooge, standing all alone, in the light that shone from one of the stained-glass windows of the church that towered over him. And with the light came the strains of *Silent Night*. George glanced up at the clock tower, where the large bronze hands showed the time to be 11.30 p.m. The carol service was about to begin and the church would soon be full of families and parishioners young and old, all waiting to celebrate the birth of the Saviour. And a tired smile formed on the old man's lips. His eyes searched the graveyard one last time for his master but Ebenezer Scrooge had disappeared from sight.

24

Ebenezer Scrooge scrambled along the path that led into the heart of the graveyard. The chill night air had helped clear his mind. He slowed down and looked up the church windows that were shedding their soft light onto the path, and heard the Christmas carols being played by the organist. "Humbug!" he hissed. He had little time for those foolish enough to celebrate what was clearly a fraud. He fished in the breast pocket of his Armani overcoat and brought out an aluminium tube with the logo Cohiba Behike on it. From his other pocket, he extracted a gold Ronson butane lighter. Shaking out the cigar, he toasted the heel (he had already guillotined the head), and bringing the cigar up to his mouth, gently sucked till the embers glowed roundly. He lifted his chin, allowing the grey smoke to trickle out into the cold night air. The nicotine in the smoke began soothing his jangled nerves. He decided to saunter down the pathway that led to the graveyard at the back of the church and away from the stream of parishioners who were beginning to make their way to the carol service.

Scrooge paused and looked back. He could make out the bright colours of the attendees as they gathered in the pool of light that formed around the open doors of the church. He could hear the scattered greetings of "Merry Christmas!" and hear the neighing laugh of the young vicar. Was he still wearing that ridiculous Christmas jumper? Scrooge mused. Feeling better and in the mood for mockery, he tiptoed back and around the edge of a large gravestone to catch a better view. To Scrooge's disappointment, the vicar was not wearing his gaudy jumper but instead white vestments with a gold sash and was beaming as he warmly greeted his parishioners. Scrooge recognised one as the owner of the large mansion on the opposite side of the square. A woman who had always greeted him with a small wave of her decrepit hand whenever he passed in his car. Wasn't there a For Sale sign outside her mansion the last time he had looked?

Scrooge took another pull on his cigar and allowed a bitter smile to play on his otherwise severe face as he watched them all troop into the church. What fools they were. Celebrating what? A fable designed solely to benefit the drinks industry, and the makers of children's toys, and the clergy? Scrooge looked at the vicar, who was throwing his head back at something the old lady had said. No doubt he'd be counting his deluded flock's money later. Scrooge took another long, satisfying pull on his cigar. At least he had not contributed to the church's annual heist.

The front of the church was now thronged with parishioners waiting to be greeted by the vicar, and Scrooge decided he would retreat into the sanctuary of the graveyard till the service began. Best not to be greeted by one of the fools who would only ask him ridiculous questions about what investments to make with their paltry sums of money. "Humbug!" he muttered again. The sight of such a collection of fools and a good hit of nicotine had all but erased the unhappy memories of his car trip back, and Scrooge's mind was already focusing on his forthcoming glass of cognac. Would he go back to his old favourite, the Rémy Martin's 1738 Accord Royal or break open a bottle of Maison Ferrand – a Christmas gift from his overpaid and underused solicitor Harry Clarke? Harry, a boring man at the best of times, had tried to impress Scrooge with his knowledge of cognac as he presented the gift. "They only use grapes grown in the Grande Champagne region," Harry had bragged. Scrooge snorted dismissively. He really could not stand such pretension. He'd go back to his favourite tipple – the Rémy Martin and then look at the Asian markets before fine-tuning his takedown of the trillionaire Von Hess.

Would it work? he mused, as he turned down the central pathway that led into the heart of the graveyard. Scrooge sucked on his cigar as he considered his chances. A lot would depend on the reaction of the markets to his gambit. He would be staking almost half his fortune on one bet and that would certainly cause a stir; not only in the markets but most certainly in the world's financial media. The money did not matter to him, just the game, and Scrooge smiled as he thought of the commotion his gambit would cause. He sucked thoughtfully on his cigar as he found himself coming face-to-face with a large granite cross. It was set in the middle of the path and marked the end of the graveyard's property. Beyond was the tall hedgerow and the outline of a mansion belonging to an Israeli industrialist. Scrooge leant up against the granite cross and paused, the cigar midway to his mouth. He had not been in these church grounds for decades. And as the strains of *Oh Little Town of Bethlehem* echoed in the air, he wracked his brain to try to recall the last time he had visited. His cigar had burnt down nearly to the head and Scrooge took delight in stubbing it out on the top of the granite cross. "One in the eye for the church," he muttered, feeling better. And then it all came tumbling back.

25

The last time Ebenezer Scrooge had visited the graveyard had been on the tenth anniversary of his mother's death. A ceremony was organised to commemorate her passing at the plot where she had been buried. Scrooge was an only child at the time and he now tried to recall whether it was to the left or right of the granite cross that he had followed his father some forty years earlier. He remembered the elaborate gravestone on the Scrooge family plot with its massive angel but little else. "Humbug!" he hissed, moving forward. The anniversary of the death of his mother which coincided, of course, with his birthday had nothing but bad memories for Scrooge, right back to the time he could first remember it. His father had always reminded him as a child that if he had not been born, his wife would still be alive. What a way to celebrate a birthday! What a way to encourage a child's sense of self-worth!

Scrooge snorted dismissively at recollections of his past birthdays. No wonder he had never visited the graveyard since. The whole episode of his birth and his mother's death were just too awful. Scorpius had often told him, throughout his childhood, that he had murdered his own mother. No wonder he hated the man!

Scrooge was now wandering up the path to the left of the granite cross when he heard something that made the skin on his neck crawl. It was like a growl of thunder, deep but distant. He looked up at the sky but it was clear of clouds of any sort. No storm there. He was alone and cloaked in darkness. So Scrooge took out his butane cigar lighter and flicked it on. There was a hiss as the strong blue flame ignited, emitting a small circle of light that allowed him to follow the pathway deeper into the shadows. Soon he could see a silhouette looming out of the murk. A couple more steps and he could make it out – the massive, brooding angel that stood guard over his mother's grave! That he did remember.

Scrooge hurried on, holding the blue flame up in front of him till he was standing before the marble angel. It towered above him, its wings outstretched, just as he had remembered it as a boy.

There was a loud noise above and a clump of snow fell at Scrooge's feet as a wood pigeon flew up from the tree beside him and over the church. Scrooge felt his heart hammer in his chest. His eyes followed the bird's flight until they came upon a light in the sky. At first Scrooge was sure it must be the taillight of a passenger plane, for it glowed red. But on closer examination, the light was not moving. Instead, it hung stationary in the air, right above Scrooge's head. "Strange," he murmured. And again the rumbling growl that this time seemed to be coming up from the ground beneath his feet.

Scrooge knelt, bringing the flame towards a polished marble plaque, and he reached forward and gently caressed the wording: **Barbara Beatrice Scrooge.**

Scrooge looked up and noticed that the light in the sky was lower, as if it had descended since he had last looked. Another growl, and this time he felt the plaque tremble under his fingers. What was it? Some underground plumbing gone wrong? His eye caught sight of another plaque that had not been there the last time he visited. He was sure of that. Scrooge held the flame up to the plaque next to his mother's and immediately his hand began to shake. It shook so badly that he dropped the lighter as he read the inscription: SCORPIUS SCROOGE.

He was standing on the grave of his father. The realisation made his bones turn to water. There was another low growl and a clear and distinct voice that seemed to come from under the ground, from the very grave of his father as it hissed "Ebenezer!"

Scrooge let out a yelp and fled. He ran through the graveyard, slipping and sliding on the ice, and made it to the rusty gate. And he did not stop until he had reached the safety of his home.

26

It was only when he had reached the elegant steps leading up to the magnificent blue double oak door of his house that Scrooge paused and took a breath. He stood for a long while looking back at the church and the adjacent graveyard. His keen eyes searching for signs, but signs of what, he asked himself. So his father had been buried there – well what of it. He had had no real dealings with his father in life so why should he be concerned about him in death. And yet… and yet… there had been those sounds and the voice calling his name and earlier the strange light in the sky over the river.

Scrooge looked at the ancient church and the stained-glass windows spilling their light into the darkness, seeking an answer. An explanation of all these weird happenings that had dogged his day. After a long moment of silence when nothing moved and no one stirred, Scrooge's worried face hardened. He was letting his imagination run wild. "Humbug," he said finally, as he turned back towards his front door. Time to stop this nonsense. He looked at the camera mounted beside the front door. It was a camera fitted with an infrared eye that scanned the human iris and only opened the door to the one person it recognised: in this case, Ebenezer Scrooge. But as he looked, Scrooge realised that infrared eye was turning into a glowing blob of plasma, the same plasma light he had seen shining over the River Thames. And the same eye that he had seen back then appeared again in the black casing, searching. The eye seemed to sense him and then it fixed him with a terrible look as a voice, deep and booming cried: "Ebenezer Scrooge!"

Scrooge turned in panic to flee but instead fell over backwards down the stairs, letting out a great cry as he hit his head on the snow-covered gravel and he knew no more.

27

For a long moment, Scrooge lay in darkness before his eyes fluttered open. In panic he pushed himself up on his elbows and searched for the infernal eye. But all he saw was the black plastic cover. No grotesque eye, no pulsating light. Scrooge struggled to his feet all the time looking at the camera. Except there was nothing to see but a black, shiny case. He felt a pounding in his head and put a finger up to his brow, feeling a sticky warmth. And when he examined his fingertips, there was a smudge of red and relief flooded his body.

"Ha!" he cried. He had imagined it all.

He clambered up the steps gingerly but when it came time to have the camera scan his eye, he held back for a split second, gazing fearfully at the camera. But all he saw was his face with a dark spot on his forehead where the blood had congealed. Scrooge inched his face closer. There was a flash of red as the infrared eye recognised his iris and the front door buzzed open.

Scrooge did not dally. Stepping through the door, he slammed it closed behind him and, bringing his eye close to the spyhole, he looked out. The empty driveway yawned back at him. The snow-covered path glinting supernaturally white in the streetlights.

"Humbug!" he said again, before disappearing up the stairs.

Ten minutes later, at exactly 11.50 p.m., Ebenezer Scrooge sat down in front of three large TV screens perched on a hi-tech glass desk. In front of him was a beautifully cut crystal brandy glass with two generous fingers of Martell XO cognac.

Scrooge was dressed in a soft silk Prada dressing gown, with matching leather slippers. There was a small plaster on his brow and another very large Cuban cigar in his hand. He raised a heavy weighted lighter and, puffing on the end of the cigar, toasted it to get it going. Then he took several long, satisfying drags, filling the large, plush office with plumes of thick blue-grey smoke. He replaced the cigar on the lead crystal ashtray and picked up the glass of cognac, circulating it luxuriously in one hand as he manoeuvred the mouse with his other.

Three different channels appeared on the three screens that flanked him. Bloomberg, MSCN, and a feed from the Shanghai Stock Exchange, Asia's biggest stock market. Scrooge sat back in his plush leather swivel chair and, cradling his drink, began to examine the graphs and the breaking news banners. The hosts of both TV stations spoke in front of a backdrop of Christmas trees and festive decorations. This was in sharp contrast to the bare grandeur of Scrooge's den, which was entirely devoid of any Christmas decorations. Not that Scrooge seemed to care. He sat sipping his cognac while puffing on his huge cigar. And all the time his eyes darted this way and that as he took in the news from the Asian markets and plotted his strategy. He did not notice the clock creeping up towards midnight and it came as a surprise, therefore, when at exactly twelve o'clock, the images on his giant TV screens froze. Then, one after the other, the screens went blank, while the table light flickered and went out, plunging the room into darkness.

Scrooge reached over and flicked the light switch on and off. Nothing. He pressed the ON/OFF switch on his computer. Nothing. He sat stock still for a moment, trying to figure out what had gone wrong. And it was while he sat in this stew of intense irritation that he first heard the noise.

28

It was the clunking of steel on concrete, as if someone was dragging a heavy chain along the ground. Scrooge remained as still as a statue, every sense in his body alert. The noise at first seemed far away. But it was growing louder. Drag… clunk… Drag… clunk… as if something or someone was pausing between each step of its progress. A progress that sounded as if it had reached the middle of his driveway.

Scrooge stood up with such violence that his chair fell backwards, hitting the floor with a mighty thump. He turned and almost tripped over the upturned chair as he made his way over to the large bay window that looked out onto the front lawn of his palatial home.

At first his hawk eyes saw nothing in the darkness, lit only by the orange streetlights. And then, from the rusty gate that led into the graveyard, he saw what looked like a ball of fog. It was thick, the height of a man, and creeping towards the front of his house. And it was from out of the centre of this fog that Scrooge heard the clank of chains.

Scrooge's eyes narrowed as he tried to pierce the impenetrable wall of fog. He felt his heart hammering in his chest. He gripped the windowsill so hard that his knuckles went white. What was happening to him? He felt a pounding in his head at each clank of the chains. Bringing up a trembling finger, he touched the plaster on his brow. Had the fall he suffered unhinged his mind? "Am I hallucinating?" he asked out loud. "That's it!" Scrooge said, pushing himself away from the window and storming out through the door. He would face whatever was outside and reassure himself – for there was nothing there. It was his scrambled, overwrought brain tricking him. He clambered down the stairs two at a time. But when he approached the front door he paused, his resolution wavering.

Under the front doorframe, small tendrils of fog were fingering their way into his house. And then came a mighty *thump,* as if a heavy chain had been dropped right outside.

Scrooge felt a strange sensation, as if his spine was liquifying. Suddenly, the power of his legs gave way and he had to hold on to the front door to keep himself upright, like a boxer holding onto the ropes after a knockout punch.

Scrooge stood, leaning against the door, every sense of his body trying to intuit what made this noise barely inches from where he stood. One, two, three seconds went by and no further sound greeted him; only a creeping cold that was travelling up his body from the floor. Looking down, Scrooge let out a strangled cry. Tendrils of fog were gathering around his ankles and reaching up to his knees. And as they wound their way around his lower leg, he felt a coldness infusing his body, a coldness that seemed to freeze the very life out of his veins.

Fighting off a rising panic, Scrooge tried to shake the fog away, as he would a small dog that had sunk his teeth into his trouser leg. But his legs had lost the power to move. Pushing down the urge to scream, Scrooge found himself face-to-face with the spyhole. He adjusted his head so that his right eye could see through the spyhole and, moving his weight forward, he looked out.

29

At first Scrooge saw nothing but a blanket of white snow. He blinked once, twice, but the scene did not change. He was about to turn when a noise rooted him to the spot. The clank of a steel chain, as if something or someone was shifting their weight right in front of him. Scrooge had to struggle not to let out a cry. He felt a tightening of the pain in his leg and, glancing down, saw that the fog had reached his thigh and had coalesced into what looked like a tight fist, holding him in its clasp. He felt an icy hand reach up to his heart. Scrooge looked through the spyhole and this time he could not hold back a howl of horror.

An eye was examining him from the other side of the spyhole. A large, bulbous, protruding eye filled with a deep intelligence and knowing. The same eye he had seen outside his front door. The same eye that had tracked him along the River Thames. But before Scrooge could do anything, he heard a voice call out.

"Ebenezer, open this door!"

And Scrooge turned pale, for he recognised the voice beyond any shadow of doubt. He opened his mouth and uttered the word he thought he would never utter again. "Father."

30

Across London, in a small one-bedroom apartment, Bobbi Cratchit was sitting on the small bunk bed and smoothing down the hair of her seven-year-old son, Tim.

Tim had been having a nightmare. His brow was a sheen of sweat and his hair matted. "Tell me about it," Bobbi had said as she held his frail body in her arms, rocking him back and forth, soothing him. Tim had awoken from a nightmare screaming hysterically. It had taken Bobbi a full two minutes to quieten him down. "Tell me, Tim."

"Okay?" Tim said finally.

"Who was scaring you?"

"Scrooge," Tim said, holding her hand lightly in his.

"Oh," said Bobbi, feeling suddenly troubled. "What happened?"

"You know the way he's mean to you, Ma?" he said, looking at his mother with two clear, blue eyes. Bobbi could not restrain a bitter laugh.

"Yes!"

"In the dream, he was running after you," Tim continued. "Throwing things at you. Shouting at you."

There was such sincerity, such conviction in the tiny voice that Bobbi's feelings of unease grew but she tried to remain calm, if only for his sake.

"Shouting what, dear?"

"He didn't want you to come back to work."

Bobbi felt her heart now hammering in her chest. How could Tim possibly know? Her desperate thoughts were interrupted by an urgent squeeze of her hand.

"Mum, is he going to fire you?"

Bobbi felt a sob rise from deep within. With a great effort, she controlled it. This wondrous child did not need to share her suffering. He had already suffered enough. Besides, she still had to explain to Tim that he could not enjoy his Christmas Day playdate with his best friend, Josh. Instead, he would have to sit all day in the office with her, while Scrooge brooded next door. That would not be fun. Not for her and certainly not for Tim.

"What's wrong, Ma?" Tim said.

"Nothing, dear." But even as she spoke, she knew he did not believe her.

"You don't look so good, Ma."

"I know," she said as stars danced before her eyes. Tim never pulled his punches. And he was right; she felt beyond exhausted. She clasped Tim to her bosom, in part to avoid his stare.

"Shush, little one," she murmured softly. Tim lay in her arms and she could feel his protruding bones.

"Oh, Ma – I had another dream. This one was better."

Bobbi held Tim at arm's length and looked into his eyes. They were filled with love.

"Tell me," she said, breathing in his love.

"There was another man in the dream. He had long hair."

And Bobbi let out an involuntary cry as she saw Jesu's face. She searched Tim's eyes.

"You saw him?" she said, terrified at what her son would reveal next.

"Yes, Ma, he's all right now but he needs your help. I think you need to find him."

Bobbi clutched her son tight again. She glanced up through the skylight window as she rocked her son gently back and forth. "Yes, we do need to find him," she said softly, feeling the outline of the silver locket in her pocket. And as her eyes grazed the clouds scudding overhead, she thought she glimpsed the light she had seen earlier. The one that had given her such comfort. And as she studied it, she noticed that its colour had changed from blue to red. But at that exact moment it went out, like a firework that was finally spent. And Bobbi felt a tremor run through her exhausted body. She placed Tim, who had fallen asleep, back on the bed and glanced at her watch.

It was exactly midnight.

31

Down in the London Docklands, a large, black rat had emerged from the pile of rubbish in the workman's hut. The snow that covered the floor made it momentarily stop and search the air, its fine whiskers probing while its feet tested the unfamiliar ice-cold white carpet. There was a sound that made its sensitive ears prick up. Something close by had stirred. Slowly, it edged forward across the snow until it came upon what looked like two objects. They were made of leather, the rat could smell that. It approached and, sniffing the leather, proceeded to follow its nose. The being was alive, the rat could sense that. There was movement in its giant body and he could smell it clearly now. The creature was rank with the smell of Thames water. Was this another form of rat? Or could this be a meal?

The rat approached the top of the long body when suddenly it stopped. A strange sensation surrounded the rat. It was like a gentle, warning heat. The rat paused. Hunger drew it on but something warned him to retreat. The hunger won out. The rat had not eaten in many long hours. It approached the place where a weak plume of breath filled the freezing air. The creature was alive. There was no doubt. Moving forward, the rat clambered over the heaving chest and approached the place where the breath came in intermittent streams. The skin of the mouth looked cracked and raw. Could this be a tasty morsel? The rat tentatively reached the place where the air came and went. It touched the raw skin with its sensitive nose and froze as the giant body stirred. At this sudden movement, the rat would usually flee but hunger made it stay. And then it saw something that made its digestive juices flow. Two blue eyes looking unblinking up into space. These indeed could offer sustenance. The rat clambered over the creature's mouth and nose till it was looking directly down at the eyes, open and unblinking. The rat bared its yellow teeth to sink into the glassy orb when it felt a sudden burning sensation on its back. It made a squeal and turned to face the assailant with its teeth still bared. But nothing was there. No other animal intent on doing it harm. Instead, far above, in a small hole in the roof, the rat caught a glimpse of a light that seemed to shine directly down on it. Without further ado, it turned and fled, back to its tunnel. Its stomach unsatisfied. Leaving the prone creature alone and bathed in a soft afterglow that shone through the hole.

32

Not a stone's throw from the worker's hut, Doctor Ellie was belting out: *Hark the Herald Angels Sing* to a dozen or so people. They were huddled around a large oil drum that was filled with burning logs of wood. Sparks flew as gusts of wind swirled and a pall of bittersweet smoke moved like a drunken dancer, pirouetting this way and that as the wind gusted, forcing coughs from those in its path and tears to spring from smarting eyes; eyes that had seen things that most people only encounter in their nightmares.

Doctor Ellie felt her phone vibrate in her pocket but ignored it. It was certainly her husband or one of her seven children demanding to know when she would be back; even though on that morning, as on all Christmas Eve mornings, she had invited them all to join her on her Christmas Eve Outreach to her homeless clients, on the wasteland down by the River Thames. Only one family member, her six-year-old Tina, had taken up her offer and Doctor Ellie now looked down as her daughter heartily joined in the singing. And Tina's presence filled Doctor Ellie with a special frisson of joy. As Doctor Ellie sang along, holding her daughter's hand and stamping her feet, she realised that she would not be anywhere else in the world.

Doctor Ellie looked out over the London Docklands and caught a glimpse of one of the soaring offices that she had visited that very afternoon – Scrooge Towers. She squinted her eyes to better make out the penthouse where she had encountered Ebenezer Scrooge.

"Scrooge!" She let out a sardonic chuckle. There was something about the name that summed up the person. It was a hard word, harsh on the lips and leaving a bitter aftertaste.

Doctor Ellie had looked up Ebenezer Scrooge online after their meeting and had been flabbergasted to see the vast estimates of his wealth. Sums of money that could never have been spent in a thousand lifetimes. Doctor Ellie was frowning when her daughter Tina squeezed her hand and nodded over at the audience.

"Ma!" she said irritably. The Christmas carol service had come to an end and the crowd was waiting expectantly for what was to happen next. Doctor Ellie's face broke into a big smile.

"Anyone for mince pies and hot chocolate?" She beamed at the gathering. There was a lot of head nodding.

"Thanks, Tina," Doctor Ellie whispered to her six-year-old. "Thanks for bringing me back to all this." She looked at her daughter and knew that she was blessed beyond belief and suddenly she felt a pang of sorrow for the childless Mr Scrooge. *I wonder what he is doing right now?*

33

At that exact moment, Ebenezer Scrooge had said a word, or tried to say a word that had not passed his lips in twenty years.

"Fa-… father?"

It was a word that was so alien to him that it actually stuck in his throat. It was a word he despised. A word he would never willingly utter and yet here he was, cowering behind the front door of his house and saying the unimaginable. Outside, beyond that door, was the sound of chains shaking. Then the door suffered a blow that made it rock on its hinges as the voice again boomed: "Open this door!"

"No!" Scrooge cried. Scrooge looked back through the keyhole. On the other side, the eye had grown, not so much in size but in the intensity of its stare. And when it saw Scrooge, a laser light exploded through the keyhole, knocking Scrooge back. There was a tremendous CRACK. The door bolts shot back and the heavy door swung open.

Scrooge cowered on his knees at the bottom of the stairs and looked up at the massive figure standing there glaring down at him.

The figure was wreathed in smoke and Scrooge could just make out a being bent over with age, the body battered and tortured out of shape.

Scrooge's eyes examined the being with a horrified fascination. The only thing keeping him from sliding into insanity was the possibility that this was somehow his father. And yet, how could that be? And was this thing even human?

There was a hollow between the top of the being's chest and chin that seemed to form a hole into nothingness. Scrooge's eyes felt the black void sucking him in, so he shifted his gaze up towards the eyes. These were the only part of the being that had colour, a glowing red. The eyes were huge, like the eyes of some grotesque goldfish. And these eyes now bored into Scrooge with an intensity that made him quail.

"What do you want with me?" Scrooge asked.

"Much!"

"Who are you?"

"You know who I am."

Scrooge shook his head. "You can't be... I don't believe any of this!"

This prompted a furious response. The being took a step into the house, raising his arms. "Tell me you know who I am!" the being demanded, shaking the heavy chains above Scrooge's head.

"You look like my father," Scrooge whispered, hardly daring to breathe. At this, the ghost made such a roar that Scrooge was forced to squirm on the ground.

"All right, all right! You are my father." And as this new reality dawned on Scrooge, his confidence returned. He had never been afraid of his father. Never! He rose slowly to his feet and faced the ghost. "You never had time for me when you were alive, so why now, when you're dead?"

There was no response, only the unblinking eye and the distant, nightmarish sounds: echoes, screams, wails. "What do you want with me?" continued Scrooge.

At this, the ghost gave his son such a look of pain that Scrooge fell silent.

"When you betray the one you are supposed to love, you suffer terrible consequences."

"Betray?"

"Yes."

There was another pause. More noises echoing in the quiet. The chains seemed to contract around the ghost, causing him to sob in pain as he nodded assent.

"And these chains?" Scrooge said, pointing a finger at the monstrous black steel links that held his father in their grip.

"I forged these link by link and yard by yard," said Scorpius Scrooge, holding them up to his son, who shrank back in horror. "You have such a chain, Ebenezer. One that is heavier and more terrible than mine."

Scrooge let out a high-pitched, nervous laugh. "I have such a thing?" he said. But the mockery stirred the ghost who rose again above him, shaking the chains in pure fury, forcing Scrooge back on his knees.

"Do not mock me, my son! There are powers at play here that you cannot comprehend!"

"What powers?" Scrooge asked but the ghost merely shook his head.

"We do not have time for this." And such was the look of agony in his eyes that Scrooge bit his lip and remained silent. "Ebenezer," the ghost continued. "I begged leave on the anniversary of my death to give you a warning."

"A warning? About what?"

"The terrible things you have done."

"What terrible things?"

"There are many."

"Such as?"

The eye of the ghost held Scrooge, the hair on his spectral head blowing back and forth in an unseen wind. "The young man whom you threw out of your office today."

"That homeless squatter – good riddance. You'd have done the same!"

"You are right, son, my life was filled with selfish acts," the ghost continued. "And now I am forced to roam the world and see my selfishness play out in the lives of those I did not help."

"Nonsense, Father, you were a good man of business."

At this, the ghost rose up again in great agitation.

"Business?" he boomed, forcing Scrooge to cower. "Humankind was my business! The common welfare was my business. Kindness. Generosity. The giving of my time. This was my business! Helping people like that young man."

"Him! Why?" Scrooge scoffed, but the eye held him in a withering stare.

"Because you never know whom you are meeting. Who they really are. But enough!" The ghost lowered his chains and came closer till his son could feel the heat emanating from his translucent flesh. "I have been granted permission to visit you, so that hearing my tale, you may change," the ghost said with such earnestness that Scrooge, who had opened his mouth to speak, closed it again. "And to that end you will be visited by three Ghosts," his father concluded.

"Three ghosts? I'd rather not," said Scrooge. "Couldn't you send them all at once and get it over with?"

"Do you want to join me in my agony?" the ghost hissed.

"I don't want to join you in anything."

"Then be warned. For your suffering will exceed mine. But enough!" it wailed. "My time is over and I must go." And with that, the ghost began to retreat towards the window, which opened, allowing him to pass through. Scrooge followed the ghost to the window.

"Father, wait!" he cried. "I have much to ask you." But Scorpius had vanished.

34

Scrooge fled his room and, taking the stairs two at a time, ran out into the garden seeking his father. And as he ran, he heard strange noises: cries, screams, shouts of alarm and wails of despair. But these sounds, for all their horror, did not lessen Scrooge's effort to pursue the ghost. He stumbled into the graveyard, panting, seeing a phantasmical ball of fog that was now gathered over the grave of Scorpius Scrooge, and in the midst of the fog, the bent over shape of his father.

Scrooge stopped dead in his tracks, watching the fog descend into the grave and he reached out a hand as the word "Father" formed on his lips. But the ghost had disappeared into the frozen ground and Scrooge stood motionless.

Behind him the hideous sounds of the underworld continued and with a sense of dread, Scrooge turned to face them. In front of him was a gathering of spirits that appeared mid-air. Ghosts that were weighed down by the chains of their misspent lives. Chains made up of money, or the trappings of fame, greed, and power.

Next to Scrooge was an old man that he recognised, a wealthy banker friend of his father's. The old man was holding an enormous iron safe, the weight of which was pulling his arms near out of their sockets. In front of him was a refugee mother, shielding her two children. Her eyes were wide with fear and her children screamed in terror. The old banker was trying desperately to open the safe. "Let me help her!" he cried, but his safe remained locked in death as it had in life.

Scrooge watched as more tales of regret unfolded around him. A rich widower with a bitter face was trying to help a destitute girl, who lay comatose on the side of a road. "Why did I send her from my house?" the old widower shrieked, as the eyes of the girl closed over for the last time. And as that ghost faded from view, Scrooge heard a spine-tingling scream and turned and saw the ghost of a soldier trying to revive a young boy. The child had a ragged hole in the side of his head. And the soldier tossed away a smoking gun and shook the young boy by his frail shoulders. "Come back, please come back!" he wailed but to no effect. Everywhere Scrooge looked were spirits trying to right the wrongs they had committed in their lives, and the air was filled with their cries and lamentations.

Scrooge clamped his hands over his ears and ran. Ran for his life. And as he passed from the graveyard, he felt the fingertips of the ghosts brush his flimsy nightgown, as if trying to grab him into their world. Scrooge let out one long scream that lasted until he reached the steps of his mansion. And there he stopped, sinking down onto his knees, gasping for breath. He looked back on the church just as the bell rang out, and everything disappeared into thin air. Scrooge felt something behind him, and heard a soft splattering sound, like a giant candle burning and spluttering in the wind. And as the last stroke of midnight echoed across the graveyard, Scrooge turned to face something beyond his imagination.

Part 2 –

The Ghost of Christmas Past

35

A young girl stood in front of Scrooge. She was dressed in a white crystal garment that seemed made up of layers of light. And the layers shimmered and shone as they moved in the midnight air. Long tussles of golden hair tumbled round slender shoulders and Scrooge noticed that her skin had a translucent quality, as if it was made of white ebony that glowed softly from within. And he saw a shimmer of flame surround her.

"What is that?" he asked, staring mesmerised at the enveloping fire. Two turquoise eyes sparkled and a smile appeared on the young lips.

"Ah," she said, "that is the power that informs me."

And with her words, the envelope of white flames wreathed around her, like the flame of a candle. And for a long moment Ebenezer Scrooge stood fascinated. Struck dumb by wonder. For unlike the ghost of his father, there were no sombre shadows or sepulchral noises that surrounded this spirit, only light. A light that shone from within and without.

"Who are you?" Scrooge murmured.

"I am the Ghost of Christmas Past."

"Whose past?"

"Your past," she said and extending a shimmering hand, added, "Come with me!"

At this, Scrooge's countenance fell as the look of wonder in his eyes was replaced by the familiar cold look of steel. "No!" he said firmly, stepping back from the proffered hand. "I will be going nowhere. I've had quite enough for one night!" And Scrooge placed both hands firmly on his hips and stuck out his chin. The Ghost made a merry noise, half laugh and half giggle, before extending her hand and grasping Scrooge's. And although he struggled with all his might, he found himself powerless.

"Hold tight!" Scrooge heard her say and he found himself being whisked off his feet and dragged upwards. He began crying out in alarm as he saw first the top of his house, then the church spire, and finally the whole of London disappearing below him. His scream turned into frightened sobs as the Ghost appeared to speed up, and soon they were travelling in a blur of light.

"Stop!" Scrooge screamed, but the Ghost did not. Instead, she turned and dragged him down a tunnel of light. "Where are you taking me?" Scrooge had to roar as he dangled from the Ghost's hand. There was no response from the Ghost. Instead, they only seemed to travel faster,

faster than the speed of light itself. Scrooge tried to close his eyes but that only made him feel dizzier. There was the sudden sound of tearing: horrible and long after which everything went quiet and Scrooge found himself hurtling down towards the ground with only the sound of the wind in his ears. He braced himself for a crash that did not materialise and instead felt his feet gently settling on the ground. The Ghost let go of his hand and he found himself standing in the shadow of an old Victorian building. Scrooge, though he recognised the building, could not exactly locate it in his memory. He looked up and down the street, searching for people or cars, but nothing disturbed the quiet of the night. He turned to the Ghost who was standing by his side, looking at him with eyes that sparkled. "I know this place but—" he said, in hushed tones. She lifted a finger for quiet and motioned to the far side of the road.

Scrooge turned to see a man exit through the open doors that spilled light onto the road. The man was carrying a small baby carrier. Scrooge found himself moving towards the figure by the sheer power of his will. He was soon travelling beside the man and saw that he was carrying a newborn baby wrapped in swaddling clothes.

He glanced at the man's face, half hidden under a black, broad-brimmed hat, and suddenly he felt a jolt.

"Scorpius!"

Scrooge followed his father and the baby and watched as they disappeared into a bank of fog. Finally, he turned back to the Ghost and raised a trembling finger. "That was where I was born." And a tear sprang unbidden from his eye. The Ghost stood in front of Scrooge and reaching out a slender finger, touched the tear, and looked at it with wonder. It glowed with a soft radiance, as if it held secrets all of its own. Then slowly it evaporated.

Scrooge continued to look at the building. "My mother lies dead in there." He said the words without emotion. Flat, monotone.

"You never knew her," the Ghost said. Scrooge remained stock still, his eyes locked on a particular window. And in the twinkling of an eye, Scrooge found himself standing outside the room, the Ghost by his side.

"You can go in."

Scrooge remained where he was, looking intently at the door. A muscle in his jaw flexed involuntarily. When he looked at the Ghost, his eyes were wide and staring.

"I never saw her," he whispered.

The Ghost nodded. "I know, but now you can." And with that, the door swung open and after a long moment, Ebenezer Scrooge stepped inside.

36

Inside the room, a nurse lifted an infant from the trembling hands of a woman drenched in sweat, her face pale and hollowed with pain. A nurse was checking the readout of the life-support instruments that the woman was attached to. She glanced up at a tall man who approached the bed. The woman lying there reached up and grabbed his hands and looked at him intensely.

"Scorpius!" she gasped, speaking through dry, cracked lips, as if every word was an excruciating effort. "Tell… our son… I… love him." The words came slowly, painfully, as if every one of them cost her dearly. Scorpius Scrooge shook his head as he clasped her hands, and tears fell freely from his eyes. "Do this for me, Scorpius…" she gasped, as the blood drained from her face.

A doctor came and laid a hand on Scorpius's shoulder but he shrugged it off angrily, more tears falling on the hands of his wife as she made one last impassioned plea.

"Do this – for me – Scorpius…" Her words were coming in long, painful gasps. "It is not his fault." And with that, she let go of her husband's hands, and her eyes rolled back in her head and the life support system emitted a long, flat beep.

Scrooge stood looking as the scene began to fade from his sight. The Ghost stood close by his side and laid a translucent, glowing hand on his shoulder; looking on as more tears welled in Scrooge's eyes and rolled down his sunken cheeks.

"He never told me…"

The Ghost nodded and, taking Scrooge by the hand, said, "We must leave this place, Ebenezer. I have more to show you."

At this, Scrooge's face contorted with rage. "No, I cannot bear this." He went to wrench his hand from hers but it was to no avail as the Ghost led Scrooge away and down another tunnel of light.

"Why do you do this to me?" he said.

"All of this is for your good." And with that, the Ghost of Christmas Past tightened her grip on Scrooge's hand as they sped on their journey.

They emerged just moments later above a heath, beside a lake. In the distance stood an imposing red brick building and Scrooge looked down to see a schoolyard looming up to meet them as they landed. The moment Scrooge set foot on the gravelled playground, his eyes were wide open with surprise. "This is my old school!" he called out excitedly.

"Yes, come," the Ghost said, leading him into one of the classrooms. And here Scrooge fell mute. For there, in a corner of the class, sitting entirely alone, was a schoolboy no older than seven or eight years of age. An open exercise book lay before him. The boy was staring out into the snow-covered playing fields. He looked utterly dejected.

"That's me!" Scrooge said, his voice tight at seeing himself so young and forlorn. At that moment, the classroom door was flung open as a young girl ran in.

"Fan!" said Young Scrooge, jumping up and running to meet her. They hugged each other and stood holding each other at arm's length. Fan was three years older than her brother and dressed in a smart red winter coat. She wore a red French beret, a knee-length black skirt, and ankle-length black boots. Her face was as warm and as bright as a red apple and her green eyes sparkled with intelligence and determination.

"I didn't think you'd be allowed to come here, Fan," said Young Scrooge.

"I nearly didn't, Eb," said Fan, tenderly touching her brother's face. "But I told Father that if he didn't invite you back to celebrate Christmas, I'd leave."

"Would you really?"

"No, but Dad believed me! He even sent me to bring you home."

Young Scrooge embraced his sister again, hugging her close as he whispered, "You're the best, Fan."

Fan disengaged from the hug and looked at him sternly.

"You promise you won't argue with him, Ebenezer."

"I can't promise that, Fan – you know that'd be a lie."

Fan held her brother's face in both hands. "I know exactly what he can be like but will you do this for me, Ebby?"

Young Scrooge nodded as a wry smile touched his face. "You always get your way, dear Fan." The two figures hugged as they faded into the mist and the ghost turned to Scrooge:

"Your sister married and had a child, did she not?"

At mention of this, the smile that had been etched on Scrooge's face disappeared. "Yes, and I wish…"

"Wish what?"

"Fred came to see me today and—"

"And?"

"I wish I had not been so…" But Scrooge's scowl soon returned. "Every year it is the same old thing – come to dinner, Uncle Ebenezer. Come and see *my wife and my brats*!"

The expression on the Ghost's face did not alter, though the envelope of flames in which she existed flared.

"Have you ever seen his… 'brats', Ebenezer?"

Scrooge shook his head violently. "Of course not!"

"Are they not your family?"

Scrooge let out a harsh laugh. "Family!" he barked, as if the word represented the worst thing on Earth. The Ghost looked long at her companion before speaking.

"Come, we must go."

"I'm not going anywhere."

The Ghost smiled and grasped Scrooge's hand again. "Time is against us."

And with that, they disappeared into another tunnel of light.

37

They entered the tunnel and this time the colours were different. More difficult for Scrooge to look at without shielding his eyes. "What is this?" he demanded of the Ghost, pointing at the colours. The Ghost turned and looked directly at him. "Your memories!"

There was a bolt of lightning and the fabric in the funnel was torn. The Ghost led Scrooge by the hand through the tear and in a moment, they were hovering above a London street. In front of them stood a large, modern building. Light spilled from windows and the sound of dance music throbbed in the air. "Do you recognise this building?" the Ghost asked, guiding Scrooge to the entrance.

"Recognise it? Of course I do!" said Scrooge, his face lighting up. "This is where I got my first job!"

The Ghost led Scrooge into a large hall. Past a plaque that read: **Fezziwig Investments.** The hall was festooned with festive lights and packed with party revellers. A large man with a florid face stood at the top of the hall on a dais next to the DJ's console. He took a mic to address the crowd.

"Why it's old Fezziwig!" said Scrooge. "I learnt so much from him." He glanced at the Ghost, his face flushed with pride. "He recognised my talent immediately."

"What talents are those, Ebenezer?"

"He said he'd never met anyone so naturally ruthless!" said Scrooge, glowing with pride.

"Ah," said the Ghost as Fezziwig began addressing the crowd.

"Thank you all for a great year," Fezziwig said. "We have made significant profits." He held up a small statuette, a sterling pound symbol covered in gold plate. "And now it is time to announce our MVP – our Most Valued Person of the Year!"

At this, Scrooge grabbed the arm of the Ghost. "Watch this!" he said excitedly. They both stood looking at the crowd, who were gazing intently at the figure of Fezziwig.

"The winner this year will need no introduction and will come as no surprise. It is the man who will no doubt conquer the world one day." He held the statuette high in the sky, where it glinted in the rotating disco lights. The crowd bayed in anticipation and the DJ played a drum roll.

"Yes," said Fezziwig, his voice mimicking one of the presenters of Fight Night as they introduced the boxers into the ring, "it is the one and only *Eb-en-e-zerrr Scr-oooo oooo-geeee!*"

The announcement was met with riotous applause and some boos.

"Always the begrudgers," Scrooge whispered to the Ghost, just as a tall, thin young man sprang up onto the stage and took the trophy from Fezziwig, who clasped him in a bear hug. Fezziwig released Scrooge and turned to the audience. "It is no secret that Ebenezer won through his iron will, grit, and determination."

"And ruthlessness!" a voice mocked from the crowd.

"Nothing wrong with a good dollop of that!" Fezziwig said, eyeing the heckler. "You could do with some of that yourself, James!" And he raised Scrooge's hand in the air, like a prizefighter.

Young Scrooge took the trophy, his young, lean face flushed with success as he spoke into the mic. "Thank you, Mr Fezziwig, and thank you all, and you, James, I love it when you hate me." He raised a finger and pointed at a very drunk member of the crowd. "And I'll see you all on the trading floor on Monday. Let's make a killing!"

The crowd roared and Young Scrooge and Fezziwig began dancing off the stage together as the DJ ramped up the music: *Money, Money, Money* by Abba. The two men began chanting the words while encouraging the audience to join in.

"Always my favourite!" Scrooge confided in the Ghost, while rocking to the music. The Ghost laid a hand on Scrooge's arm. "Come, Ebenezer, we have more to see."

"Oh," said Scrooge, his smile fading, "I was enjoying that."

38

The Ghost led Scrooge to the adjoining room, where the younger Scrooge was queuing up to order a glass of wine. The Ghost brought Scrooge up to the counter so that he was looking over the shoulder of his younger self. Suddenly Scrooge stopped dead in his tracks and his face went as white as a sheet.

"Take me from here!" he hissed at the Ghost, his whole body trembling. "Take me from here!" he repeated again in a low, venomous voice.

"What is it, Ebenezer?" the Ghost asked but Scrooge could not form words with his lips. Instead, he raised a trembling finger and pointed at the young woman who was serving the wine.

She was in her very early twenties. A woman of remarkable beauty. She had long raven black hair and large, brown eyes. She wore a knee-length black skirt over a crisp white summer shirt that covered her hourglass shape. And this stunning creature seemed to have captivated the younger Scrooge, who was looking at the waitress rapturously as he waited to be served.

But the older Scrooge remained horrified. And when he turned to face the Ghost his face was riven with anguish.

"Take me from here!" he insisted. The Ghost held him steadily in her gaze.

"These are the shadows of things that happened, Scrooge. You cannot change them."

"But I do not have to suffer them. Take me from here!" The Ghost held a hand over Scrooge's head and a gentle light fell on his desperate countenance.

"You must endure this, Ebenezer," she said. "That is the purpose of my visit."

Scrooge fell silent and looked on as his younger self reached the top of the queue and accepted a glass of wine. And as the waitress handed it over, she noticed the statuette.

"You won something?" she asked, her brown eyes sparkling.

"I did," said Young Scrooge. "But I'd like to win something else tonight. What is your name?"

"Belle." The face of Young Scrooge broke into a huge smile.

"Belle means beautiful, how appropriate."

Belle nodded and smiled. By now a queue had formed as Scrooge got some catcalls. "Belle, will you join me for a drink later? After your work is finished."

Belle narrowed her eyes as she looked at the young man in front of her. She tilted her head one way and then the other, as if considering the matter.

"Go on!" said Young Scrooge. "Just a drink."

"Okay," she said finally.

The scene changed to outside the party and Scrooge found himself listening in as the young couple, wine glasses in hand, chatted on the stone steps at the back of the building.

"You're ambitious?" Belle asked.

"I think you can say that," Young Scrooge answered. His eyes never leaving Belle's face.

"What's more important to you: money or love?" Her eyes twinkled as she asked the question, her head again tilting at an angle, as if to better see her companion. He reached out and took her hand in his.

"Before tonight I would have said money." He looked deep into her eyes. "But now I am not so sure."

Belle took her hand out of his. "Not so sure?" she said in mock protest. Gently, Young Scrooge took her hand back and held it softly in both of his.

"No, I am sure and I choose love!" he said, leaning forward and trying to kiss her. But she moved her face away.

"In my country—" she began.

"What country is that?"

"Brazil of course, did you not guess?"

Young Scrooge smiled. "Go on."

"In my country we say 'o vinho fala'."

"Let me guess," said Young Scrooge. "The wine does the speaking?"

She clapped her hands. "Very good – you speak Portuguese?"

"A little, but I do speak fluent French, a smattering of Italian, just enough German to get by, and some Russian!"

"I'm impressed," said Belle and this time it sounded as if she meant it. Young Scrooge brought her hand up to his lips and gave it the softest of kisses.

"I don't need wine to see my future," he said simply. Belle laughed and again removed her hand from his.

"And what is your future Mr Ee-ban-ezer?" she asked, drawing out the words so they both laughed.

"I believe I am looking at it," he said, and he took her hand yet again and this time she did not take it back.

Standing behind them, Old Scrooge let out a long groan of pain. "Ghost, remove me from this place," he said.

"Not yet!" the Ghost said and the scene changed again.

39

Young Scrooge and Belle were sitting on a blanket. It was a summer's day and a picnic was laid out before them on the grass. Belle was snuggled up close to Young Scrooge, dipping plump, red strawberries in a cream tub and feeding them to him as his head lay in her lap. She stopped and looked up at the sky, shaking out her long locks of dark raven hair. She was dressed in a summer frock and her long legs and arms were the colour of a deep coffee. She wore no make-up but such were the fineness of her features that her beauty shone through.

"Ebby," she said, running a finger around the curve of his lean cheek. "Can such happiness as ours last?"

Young Scrooge sat up. "It can and it will," he said, leaning over and kissing her. She held the kiss long, cradling his face with both her hands.

"I just have a feeling," she said finally, placing both hands in her lap.

"You do?" he said with a mischievous smile. "So do I! Close your eyes."

Belle tilted her head as she looked at her beau, and realising he was serious, she closed her eyes. When she opened them again, he was holding up an engagement ring. It was a large, single diamond that caught the rays of the sun. Belle's hand flew to her mouth. "What is this, Ebby?"

Young Scrooge got up onto one knee and, offering the ring to Belle, said, "Will you marry me?"

Belle stared at the ring that glittered with sunlight.

"Are you serious?"

"Never more serious in all my life," he answered.

She smiled and nodded. "Of course I will, Ebby!" And he placed the ring on her finger. Belle held the ring up to the sunlight as tears of joy filled her eyes.

"It's beautiful," she said, drawing her lover in for a passionate kiss.

"And now for the difficult part," said Young Scrooge, looking at his fiancée. "How to break the news to my father!"

"Surely he'll be delighted for you?"

"Ha," Young Scrooge exclaimed, as they began packing away the picnic. "My father doesn't think I deserve to be happy."

Belle frowned. "That's a terrible thing to say, Ebby."

"He's a terrible man."

The two lovers disappeared into the mist and Old Scrooge let out a cry of pain like that of a wounded animal. The Ghost of his Past looked sternly at Old Scrooge. "You must relive the past, Ebenezer, if you are to reclaim the future. Come, follow me."

40

Scrooge and the Ghost re-emerged from the fog to find themselves standing in a large study. Behind a desk sat Ebenezer's father, Scorpius Scrooge. He had become a stout man and had a frown on his florid face. He was dressed in a plush red velvet smoking jacket and his small, pig-like eyes looked at the young couple sitting opposite him with grave disapproval. A glass of whiskey sat before him, though the clock behind showed that it was just two o'clock in the afternoon. There was a long, uncomfortable silence.

"We won't have a drink, Father, but thanks for offering," said Young Scrooge pointedly.

"Still as sarcastic as ever!" Scorpius said sharply, lifting the glass in an unsteady hand and knocking the contents back. Belle, who had entered with a friendly smile glanced uncertainty at her young lover. He took her hand in his and smiled warmly back at her, causing Scorpius to shift uncomfortably in his chair. "Well?" Scorpius snapped, refilling his glass from a heavy crystal decanter. "What do you want?"

"May I introduce you to Belle, my fiancée."

Scorpius almost dropped his glass. "Your what?"

The jaw muscles of Young Scrooge flexed but he held the smile on his face.

"Belle," he repeated, slowly as if speaking to a child, "the woman I am going to marry."

The small pig-eyes flicked from one face to the other. "Marry?" he repeated, slurring his words, "You are going to marry this…" His eyes looked Belle up and down. "Why, she's not even…"

"Not even what, Father?" said Young Scrooge, the smile disappearing entirely from his face.

"She's not one of us."

Belle was staring at Scorpius but her smile had disappeared. Young Scrooge renewed the grip on her hand as his jaw muscles flexed.

"Father, let me be clear," he said, keeping his voice steady, though his cheeks flushed red. "I am marrying Belle. You can join our celebration or not. That is your choice. But it won't make a difference to our decision."

Scorpius Scrooge stood with such force that he knocked the whiskey glass over, the contents spilling across the desk.

"Marry this woman and you will no longer be part of my family."

Young Scrooge stood, his eyes burning into those of his father.

"I have never been a part of your family. Not from the moment I drew breath. You have always believed that I killed Barbara and you have punished me since the moment I was born."

Young Scrooge looked across at Belle, who was now standing by his side. "I have found true love, Father, and I am not going to let it go." He squeezed Belle's hand and she squeezed back as tears welled in her eyes. Scorpius Scrooge turned his furious gaze on her.

"You think you can take my son from me?" he said, spit speckling his lips as he spoke, the smell of whisky strong off his breath.

"I am not taking anything," Belle said, her voice trembling with emotion. "I am giving myself to your son, to your family."

Scorpius Scrooge's lip twisted in a contemptuous sneer.

"Very clever, very clever," he hissed, "but I know your sort. You have ensnared my son for one reason only."

"What's that?" Belle said, her eyes challenging the man who stood threateningly before her.

"His money."

Belle shook her head in disbelief as Young Scrooge put a protective arm around her. "Believe what you like, it will make no difference," he said, taking Belle's hand and turning to leave.

"How dare you turn your back on me," Scorpius said to Belle. "I have not finished."

Young Scrooge continued to walk away but Belle stopped and turned to face Scorpius.

"Yes?" she said.

The pig-eyes of Scorpius Scrooge narrowed. "You will regret ever having met my son."

Belle held his stare before turning and taking Young Scrooge's hand. They left the room together and the image faded, leaving Ebenezer Scrooge and the Ghost alone in the darkness.

41

The Ghost of the Past turned to Scrooge, who was staring ashen-faced at the spot where the vision had faded.

"Why are you showing me this?" Scrooge said. "I know what happened!"

"No, you don't, Ebenezer. Not all of it, sadly."

"What do you mean?"

"Come," said the Ghost, turning to leave.

"I'm not going anywhere!"

"You must and you will if you are to save yourself." The light from her young eyes burned bright, entering the pupils of Ebenezer Scrooge and illuminating his mind. And it seemed that his face changed and his slumped shoulders righted themselves.

"I will try," he said finally.

She reached out a hand and this time Scrooge took it. And soon they found themselves in Belle's humble home. Young Scrooge's wedding suit was hanging on a stand and he was trying on his matching grey top hat.

"I look ridiculous!" Young Scrooge said, taking off the top hat and tossing it on the bed.

"No!" squealed Belle in mock horror, retrieving the hat and placing it on his head. "You look handsome!" She turned him towards the mirror and they stood in silence as they both took in the sight before collapsing on the bed in laughter. Belle was the first to extract herself from what had turned into a passionate embrace.

"You have to leave, Ebby."

"Why?" he asked, stroking strands of hair back from her face, his eyes filled with love and longing.

"You know the bride cannot stay with the bridegroom on the night before their wedding."

"Superstitious nonsense!" Young Scrooge said. "We'll be man and wife tomorrow."

"So what's another day?" said Belle mischievously, extricating herself from the embrace and sitting up on the bed. Suddenly, her face became serious. "I had a dream about your father last night, Ebby."

Young Scrooge's smile disappeared as if he had been slapped. "Belle, we agreed not to mention his name."

"I know," Belle said, taking his hand in hers. "But it frightened me."

Young Scrooge put his hands on his fiancée's shoulders.

"Whatever he threatens, he cannot stop us," he said. But still the shadow of doubt remained on Belle's face. She looked down into her lap, shaking her head.

Placing a finger under Belle's chin, Young Scrooge lifted her face till their eyes locked. "I place my life in your hands," he said. "Not tomorrow but now. Right now."

Tears welled in Belle's eyes and Old Scrooge, who was looking on from the side of the bed, let out a sound somewhere between a sob and a cry. "I cannot bear this," he whispered but the Ghost laid her small hand on his shoulder.

"You can and you will, now watch!"

Old Scrooge turned back to the scene unfolding on the bed just as Belle placed a hand on her young lover's cheek.

"I place my life in your hands, Ebenezer." Then her eyes narrowed, as if she had received an insight. "And know this: I will always be yours, whatever happens. You understand?"

A look of doubt appeared in Young Scrooge's eyes.

"'Whatever happens?' What do you mean?"

"Just know I would never betray you. Whatever happens, know that."

Young Scrooge searched Belle's eyes, a look of doubt being suddenly replaced by a look of pure longing. And taking Belle's face in both his hands, he kissed her with a passion that she had not experienced before. At first she resisted, gently trying to prise herself from her lover's embrace. And then, realising something unseen and unspoken had occurred, she returned his kisses with a passion that exceeded even his. And they sank onto the bed in an embrace that signalled that they had both accepted they were now husband and wife, forming one body and one soul.

42

The scene changed and Scrooge found himself beside the Ghost of his Past, looking on as his younger self stood at the altar, dressed in the morning suit and holding his grey top hat under his right arm. Behind him the aisles of the small church were packed with relatives and friends, all decked in their best wedding outfits. Young Scrooge looked nervously at his best man, who checked his wristwatch.

"It's only forty minutes, Ebby. My wife kept me waiting an hour," the best man whispered.

But the frown did not leave Young Scrooge's face. He tried to smile at the small band of Belle's Brazilian friends sitting in the front row, all decked out in their best and most colourful finery. They beamed back at him, giving him the thumbs up. A head suddenly appeared around the church door and cried, "She's coming!" There were murmurs of excitement and Young Scrooge turned to his best man. "Wait here!" He hurried down the aisle and exited the church, exchanging the shadows for the bright sunshine outside.

A blue and grey Rolls Royce Phantom was driving up the long avenue that led to the church. White ribbons decorated the front of the car. They fluttered noisily in the wind as the car swept up beside Young Scrooge and came to a crunching halt in the gravel. The driver got out and went to open the door but the smile of relief on Young Scrooge's face disappeared in an instant. For the person that got out of the car was not Belle, but the last person on Earth that the young Ebenezer Stooge had expected to see on his wedding day.

43

Scorpius Scrooge stepped out of the Rolls Royce and stood looking at his son Ebenezer. The young man pushed roughly past his father and thrust his head into the back of the car. It was empty.

"Where is she?" He turned on his father; his face was flushed red, his hands turned into fists. Scorpius held up a hand but did not take a step back.

"Prepare yourself for bad news, son."

Scrooge stepped right into his father's face. "Where is she!" he roared.

"Read this," Scorpius said, reaching into his jacket pocket and handing his son a document. Young Scrooge snatched it and began reading, and as he did so, his face drained of colour.

"A warrant – for her arrest?" Young Scrooge said, and shoving the document back into Scorpius's hands, he grabbed the lapels of his father's jacket. "If you have done anything to her, I'll kill you."

Scorpius Scrooge did not resist his son's attack. Instead, he said softly, "I have done nothing to your precious Belle. It's what she has done to you, Ebenezer." A police car, its siren wailing, appeared racing up the driveway towards them. "They will tell you the truth." Scorpius added, as the police car pulled up and braked hard behind the Rolls Royce. A plain-clothes police officer got out and approached the two men. "This is my son Ebenezer, officer," Scorpius Scrooge said.

"I'm Detective Paul Tomson from the Fraud Squad," the officer said, looking intently at Young Scrooge.

"What has happened to my fiancée?"

"Belle Santiago?"

"Yes."

The officer glanced over to Scorpio, who nodded.

"The bank alerted your father this morning that Ms Santiago had transferred all the money from your bank account into her account in Brazil. We tried to contact you first, Mr Scrooge, but you were understandably busy, so the bank put us in contact with your father."

"She couldn't have done," said Young Scrooge, his voice trembling.

"Sadly, she did." Officer Tomas continued, "Every penny's gone."

"It gets worse, I'm afraid," said Scorpius. "She was spotted on a plane taking off to Rio de Janeiro just over an hour ago."

Young Scrooge looked from his father to the police officer, who nodded. "My colleagues in Border Control just rang and confirmed it. We were too late to arrest her. And when she lands in Rio, we cannot touch her. There's no agreement in place between our two countries."

For a long moment, Young Scrooge looked wildly from the police officer to his father, his mouth opening and closing like a fish. Then he sprang. "You're behind this!" he screamed as he grabbed his father by the throat. The police officer separated them as the guests from inside the church began gathering around them.

"I'm so sorry," Scorpius said, as the police officer and the best man restrained Young Scrooge. Scorpius, now freed, stepped forward to address the wedding guests. "I'm so sorry to have to say there will be no wedding." There were cries of dismay. "Why?" came the echoes.

"It appears the bride has run off to Brazil with all my son's money," said Scorpius. There were wails of disbelief and cries of "That's a lie!" and "She'd never do that!" as the police stepped forward.

"I must tell you that a warrant has been issued for Ms Santiago's arrest. Does anyone know her whereabouts?"

There were shouts of disbelief.

"I'm so sorry—" Scorpius said, addressing the wedding guests.

"You're not sorry," Young Scrooge interrupted, stepping in front of his father. "You said you'd stop her from marrying me."

Scorpius Scrooge turned to face his son.

"Ebenezer, you are right. I did not want you to marry her because I knew what she was after. And I was proved right, though it pains me to admit it."

There were more cries of dissent from some of the guests but Scorpius raised the police warrant in the air. "The truth is Belle stole everything from my son," he said, turning back to face his son, "and even as you were waiting here to marry her, she was boarding a plane to Rio." There were gasps from the guests but Scorpius continued, "She betrayed you, Ebenezer. She betrayed you all but I am still here."

Scorpius went to hug his son but was pushed violently away.

"No, Ebenezer!" the best man shouted, grabbing his friend. Scorpius held up a hand for silence and turned to his son.

"Ebenezer, you rejected me for her. And she betrayed you and rendered you penniless. I will forgive you," he continued. "I'll even offer you back your job – share my home with you. Welcome you back to our family – your only family." He opened both his arms towards his son, drawing words of approval from some of the guests. "Come back to me."

Young Scrooge's face was riven with despair. A friend of Belle's came over to embrace him but he pushed him angrily away. He turned to his father, who still had his arms wide open to receive him. But instead, he spat on the ground at his father's feet.

"You are dead to me," he said, and turning on his heel, he walked away.

44

After the scene had dissolved, Scrooge stood in the darkness and when he did finally speak, his words were uttered in a hushed, pleading tone. "No more, Spirit."

The Ghost of Christmas Past took Scrooge gently by the hand and led him forward to a place suddenly filled with bright sunshine and throbbing with vibrant life. And though at first Scrooge closed his eyes and shook his head, the warmth of the sun and throb of life finally made him open them. And there was a look of recognition.

"I know this place," Scrooge said, looking up at the ragged, dishevelled hovels that passed for houses. The Ghost and Ebenezer Scrooge walked forward hand-in-hand, unseen by the milling crowds. And they were soon swallowed up in a chaotic mix of people, cars, bikes, buggies, and noise, as the life of a Brazilian favela throbbed them.

"I remember this place," said Scrooge and before the Ghost could answer, a familiar figure appeared before them. It was Young Scrooge dressed in a T-shirt, shorts, and flip-flops, walking all alone in the Brazilian favela. He was a changed man. His face was leaner, harder, and etched with the first lines of age and care. He was showing a photo to a group of locals who had gathered around him. The Ghost led Scrooge closer till they could see that the photo he was holding was of Belle.

Some of the locals pointed to the road behind, another to a block of flats. "You never found her," the Ghost said, turning to Scrooge, who shook his head, his eyes suddenly angry.

"I needed to hear her confess her betrayal with her own lips. But I never found her."

"Come," said the Ghost, who took Scrooge's hand and led him into a house on the far side of the square. It was a small apartment but one that was well tended. A place that looked down on the very spot where Young Scrooge had been showing his photo to the locals. They entered the small bedroom overlooking the square and Scrooge stopped dead in his tracks.

Sitting on a sofa sat Belle. She was cradling a small infant, wrapped in a blue blanket. She looked the same but different, a mixture of joy and sorrow. His eyes fell on the baby's head and a tuft of raven black hair peeked out at him. The shadow of someone entering the room fell across mother and baby and a young man entered, carrying a bottle of baby milk. He was tall, also with jet-black hair and gentle, brown eyes that looked on lovingly as he leant over and kissed the head of the baby while handing the bottle to Belle.

Scrooge turned on the Ghost, his face white as a sheet.

"Take me from here!" he commanded.

The Ghost held up her hand. "Ebenezer, this is not what you think it is."

"Oh yes it is; she betrayed me for him!" He pointed angrily at the young man. "My father was right. Take me from HERE!"

There was an explosion of light and the sound of time and space tearing open.

"No, Scrooge, wait," the Ghost said, reaching out a hand.

"Never!" Scrooge commanded. And with the image of Belle, the baby, and her lover imprinted on Scrooge's brain, he broke violently away with a great effort of will and fell into darkness, leaving the Ghost of the Past behind him.

Part 3 –
The Ghost of Christmas Present

45

In London, the bells of St. Paul's Cathedral were ringing out in celebration as Christmas Day arrived in a flurry of snow. Across the River Thames, and shrouded in a swirl of snowflakes, the peregrine falcon was similarly alert, its great discs of eyes searching the sky. And such was the power of its vision that it made out a rent in the clouds above. Blinking once, it cocked its head as the two eyes focused in on the gap. Something was reflected in the shiny orb of its eye. A distillation of light falling. Something or someone hurtling back down to earth.

The falcon stood and flexed its wings, shedding the particles of fine snow that had gathered there, before launching off from the top of the tall chimney and flying high into the sky. And as it flew, it made a beeline for the spot where the object was falling, twisting and turning in the air as it went. And the great bird followed, hunting down the falling object as it would its prey, before landing on the spire of a church that stood next to a palatial house shrouded in darkness. The light had disappeared into the great house that was shrouded in darkness, apart, that is, from one room at the front, which glowed with a soft, otherworldly light.

The falcon alighted from the spire and swooping down, settled on the windowsill of the room into which the falling object had disappeared. And there it looked in, searching, until it saw the shape of a man lying on the floor. The bird looked up and noted an approaching figure that glowed orange and shed purple light all around it. The falcon shuffled its giant claws on the windowsill and excitedly pecked its razor-sharp beak on the window. The orange light within the room flared softly at the noise and bathed the falcon in a gentle glow. The peregrine falcon raised its head in what looked like acknowledgement and alighted from the window, taking just one beat of its powerful wings to return and resume its vigil on the nearby church spire. Its two eyes never leaving the soft glowing light.

46

Ebenezer Scrooge let out one long cry as he fell in the darkness before landing with a thump on his own floor. A small, insistent tapping sound made him open his eyes and glance up. And what he saw there made him doubt his sanity. For a fully grown bird of prey was on the other side of the windowpane and looking in with large, unblinking eyes.

Scrooge raised his head from the carpet to better see the bird. And as he did so, the bird blinked and inclined his head, and in the shiny orb of its right eye, Scrooge saw clearly the reflection of an orange light. At this, the bird flapped its wings and disappeared.

Scrooge propped himself on his elbows and turned to look behind him and let out a sharp exhalation of breath. Standing in front of him was an enormous woman all of eight feet tall. She was dressed in a baggy Christmas jumper, which had the inscription: ENJOY XMAS WHILE YOU CAN! emblazoned across the front in electric letters that flashed red and white. The baggy jumper came down to her knees which, together with her massive legs, were covered in luminous, lime-green tights – a hideous sight to Scrooge's exhausted eyes. The being had two enormous feet that were shod in large white runners that sparkled with lights as she moved her feet from side to side. Scrooge looked back at her face and saw that her lips were humming the John Lennon classic: "So This is Christmas." Scrooge examined the large face that was framed by a cascade of orange hair was kept in place by a pointed Santa cap. But it was the eyes that held Scrooge's entire attention, for the two pupils kept changing colour. From orange to purple and back to crimson and pink and orange again. And the eyes, like the voluptuous mouth below it, crinkled with an outlandish smile, while laughter bubbled up from deep within, filling the room with a bright sound that echoed off the ceilings and floor.

"You must be Ebenezer Scrooge!" she said, her voice cracking with laughter.

"I am," said Scrooge, immediately on edge at the high-pitched guffawing. "What's so funny?"

At this, the apparition doubled over in laughter. Laughter that did not appear to be stopping anytime soon. "Well?" Scrooge snapped, clambering with some difficulty up off the floor. Still no answer, only more laughter. "What's so FUNNY?" he screamed.

The large woman gradually brought her mirth under control and regarded Scrooge with mocking eyes.

"With all your gazillions you are still the unhappiest soul I have ever had the dis-pleasure of meeting!" she said, before laughing again till the tears ran down her face.

"Let me speak plainly," Scrooge said, his voice terse. "I've had a difficult few hours. So, can you tell me exactly who you are so we can get on with" – he paused, as he struggled to find the word – "whatever it is you have planned?"

The apparition wiped away tears with the back of a chubby hand and took a couple of deep breaths to calm herself.

"Ebenezer, I'm the Ghost of Christmas Present and I have much to show you!"

"That's a pity," he said waspishly. "But I have learnt it is near impossible to resist."

But even as he said this, his mind was taken back to the Rio favela and the way he had left the Ghost of Christmas Past high and dry. He eyed the laughing Ghost, his eyes suddenly filled with cunning. Perhaps he could also give this Spirit the slip.

"Not a chance, Scrooge," laughed the Ghost. "You can put that silly little thought right out of your head!" And she gave Scrooge a hearty slap on the back that nearly knocked him off his feet. "You dealt badly with my sister spirit so don't try it on with me! I'm not quite as forgiving."

She laughed and gave Scrooge another slap. "And you didn't allow my sister to show you your full story." Then she wagged a finger in Scrooge's face.

"I'd heard quite enough," said Scrooge bitterly.

"And what did you hear, poor Ebenezer?" the Ghost said mockingly. Scrooge's face darkened.

"I heard that I was betrayed by a woman who took all my money and ran off with another man. Oh, and she had a baby with him." His face was like a cut lemon. "Nearly forgot that small detail."

The Ghost looked long at Scrooge, all the time her eyes shifting colour at a dizzying rate. "You sure she abandoned you, Ebenezer?"

"Yes."

"Really?" the Ghost said, shaking her head. "Perhaps you should have stayed till the end to hear the full story my sister had to tell."

"And be more humiliated – no thanks."

The eyes of the Ghost turned bright red. "Maybe you wouldn't have been humiliated, maybe you would have been enlightened. But" – she shrugged her huge shoulders – "the Past is not my business."

"And what exactly is your business?" said Scrooge.

"The present – your present – best buckle up your seat belt, Ebenezer!"

"Buckle up? What are you talking about?"

"If you found your past upsetting, it's nothing compared to your present!" The Ghost chortled, her large Christmas jumper suddenly flashing its message: ENJOY XMAS WHILE YOU CAN!

In the flash, they had moved through the wall and were standing outside Scrooge's home. On the driveway was parked an old dilapidated Vespa scooter. It was faded pink and its paint was peeling, revealing large areas of rust, while the fake-leather seat was ripped open, the foam padding erupting from inside.

"Hop up now," said the Ghost, straddling the machine and starting the engine, which coughed black smoke.

"On that?"

"Yes. It may not be that fancy limo of yours but it will do."

With an audible sigh, Scrooge clambered on board behind the huge figure, who turned and looked down at him.

"And I hope you treat this driver with more respect than poor old George."

"How do you know about him?"

"You'd be surprised what I know, Scrooge. Now grab hold of my jumper!"

With a sigh, Scrooge reached out a hand, but before he had even touched the green material, there was a whoosh of noise and a rush of wind as the Vespa took off like a rocket.

47

As the Vespa took off, Scrooge nearly fell off and he was forced to hold onto the Ghost. He was hard pressed, for the Ghost flung the Vespa this way and that, defying the laws of physics and the oncoming traffic. Scrooge eventually got a hold of the Ghost's Christmas jumper, which smelt of pine needles and glowed with a soft but potent energy. Soon they braked hard and Scrooge found his face squarely planted into the Ghost's back. For a split second, he disappeared into what appeared to be a force field of pure orange energy, before his face came out like a cork from a Champagne bottle.

"You alright, Scrooge?" The Ghost chortled, stepping off the scooter as Scrooge toppled to the ground.

"You care?" he spat, dusting himself off. He looked up to find himself outside a suburban house. It had a dilapidated garden and seemed in dire need of a lick of paint. But what it lacked in upkeep it more than made up for in Christmas cheer.

The front of the house was bedecked in Christmas lights, while the garden gnome was dressed in Santa's costume, its lights flashing on and off, as it stood guard by the front gate, which was hanging from its hinges.

The Ghost parked her Vespa and motioned Scrooge to follow her up the icy garden path, all broken paving stones, overgrown with weeds. Scrooge peered at a front door, which was also in need of a coat of paint. "Why do you bring me here, Ghost?"

"Surely you know who lives here?" asked the Ghost, raising an orange eyebrow. Scrooge shook his head.

"Sorry, but I don't know the kind of people who live in this kind of place."

"Shame on you, Scrooge," the Ghost said, delivering another thunderous slap on the back. "Why, it's your nephew Fred and his family." The Ghost bought her bulging eyes close to Scrooge's so he could feel the heat of her gaze. "Remember them, Scrooge – your *only* living family!"

Scrooge felt suddenly uncomfortable. "I'm sure they don't want to see me," he said, backing back up the path. "They'll have presents to pack or whatever it is that families do at Christmas."

The Ghost let out a laugh and another slap (not so hearty this time) landed on Scrooge's back. "Enough of your nonsense – follow me!"

They entered the house by simply walking through the walls and Scrooge finally met the family he had avoided all his life.

48

A scene of Christmas chaos greeted Scrooge. Kids of multiple shapes and sizes running from room to room, each emitting shrill shrieks, whoops, and roars of delight. All seemed on a mission but to where was totally unclear to Scrooge's uninitiated eye. Many carried things in their hands or under their arms. Some dragged objects, others pushed, some pulled while all the time speaking in shrill, piercing voices that made Scrooge clamp both hands over his ears. The inside of the house was bursting with Christmas decorations of every shape, colour, and size. There was a magnificent Christmas tree that seemed to be tilting alarmingly to one side, like an arboreal tower of Pisa. A roaring fire lit up the living room where they now stood. Everywhere was festooned with every kind of decoration: flashing strings of Christmas lights and candles and a collection of Christmas cards that hung suspended on a piece of string over the fireplace, the vectored heat making them dance manically.

Into the room came the lady of the house, Fred's wife Donna, carrying a tray laden down with glasses of hot chocolate and two empty pewter mugs. Fred followed his wife into the room brandishing a red-hot poker. He was followed Pied Piper like, by a line of excited children from three years of age to thirteen and beyond.

"Show us, Dad!" voices cried as Fred removed a small black iron cauldron that had been sitting in the flames.

"Careful now, kids – we don't want any accidents!"

He placed the cauldron on a low table next to the fire and with a flourish, plunged the red-hot poker into the frothing liquid that was bubbling away. There was a mighty hiss and steam erupted from the cauldron, drawing squeals of delight from the children.

Fred accepted a pewter mug handed to him by his older daughter Pam, a lithe sixteen-year-old with her mother's golden hair and her father's intelligent, mocking eyes. Fred offered the steaming mug to his wife and then served himself a mug of the hot, steaming punch while the kids took up their cups of hot chocolate.

"An extra marshmallow to anyone who can name Mum's favourite movie," Fred said, lifting a tray of toasted marshmallows from the fire. A chorus of *It's a Wonderful Life* filled the air, forcing Old Scrooge, who was near the centre of the room, to cover his ears again.

"Come on, Scrooge," the Ghost mocked, "none of your amateur dramatics!"

Fred, meanwhile, was dealing with multiple claims on the marshmallow reward.

"You know what I'll do?"

"What!" roared the company of kids.

"As I can't decide, I'll give each one of you an extra marshmallow." This was greeted with more cries of delight, forcing Scrooge to reinsert his fingers again as Fred raised a hand for quiet.

"But you'll only get your treat if you leave now – agreed?" The room was emptied before the words were fully out of Fred's mouth. He handed the tray of marshmallows to Kate and gave her a peck on the cheek. "I don't intend to see any one of you till after the movie, understand?"

"Promise, Dad!" said Kate before disappearing from the room.

Fred collapsed next to Donna on the sofa. "You did well, husband," Donna said, patting Fred's arm.

"Thank you, my dearest. But we really don't expect them to keep that promise, do we?" Fred laughed, lifting his glass to take a swig. But he paused halfway. "I've got an idea; let's make a toast."

"Yes, dear, to us?"

Fred shook his head as he turned to his wife.

"No, let's toast Uncle Scrooge!"

The smile on his wife's face disappeared instantly. "Fred, no!"

But Fred only laughed out loud. "Ha, if you'd only seen him this morning."

"That's the problem. I never do see him. We never see him," said Donna, her face suddenly sour.

"Oh, come on now—"

"Come on you!" she replied angrily. "Has your uncle been to even one birthday celebration for the kids?" Fred shook his head. "Or one Christening? Has he ever even *seen* our kids?" Fred shook his head again as Donna's face flushed with fury. "It's not like he has any other relatives or any other friends, for that matter. And you traipse up to his office every Christmas for what?" She looked at her husband, whose chuckling had subsided. "To be insulted?" His wife continued shaking her head. "I just won't have it, Fred, and that's the end of it."

"You right, he's insufferable," said Fred, leaning against his wife and taking a swig from his still steaming mug. "But for all that, I feel sorry for him."

"I don't," said Donna, bristling. "I think he's a creep."

Fred remained thoughtful. "You know," he said, squeezing his wife's hand. "When I looked at him today, I got the oddest feeling."

"Yes?" Donna said, looking closely at her husband, noting the change in his demeanour. "What feeling?"

Fred sighed. "I had the feeling this could be his last Christmas. And what a waste that would be – dying without family or friends…"

Donna looked anything but happy at this statement.

"Your uncle had ample opportunity to start a family."

"Really?" said Fred looking perplexed, before his face lightened. "Ah, you mean the beautiful Belle."

Old Scrooge started in alarm at this turn in the conversation but the Ghost laid a restraining hand on his arm. "Steady now!" she whispered.

"I often wonder what really happened there?" Donna continued.

"Between my uncle and Belle?" said Fred.

"Yes," said Donna, turning to her husband. "You knew her; was she a gold digger? Did she really run off with his fortune?"

"Ha, now there's a question!" said Fred, settling back to relive an old memory.

49

"I only met Belle that one time and she seemed like a very nice person. But you know what money does to people."

"Yes!" laughed Donna. "Look at your uncle!"

Old Scrooge started to open his mouth in protest, only for a look from the Ghost to quiet him as Fred continued.

"I was very young at the time, but I still remember the wedding."

"You were there?"

"Yes, I was a groom's boy. I was carrying the rings to the altar! In fact—" Fred put a hand on his forehead at the realisation. "I believe I still have them somewhere."

"What, the rings?" said Donna, open-mouthed.

"Yes. You see, there was such a commotion when the wedding was called off and the police arrived and no one was worried about wedding rings! I was just bundled straight home."

"Yes, I suppose that would happen," said Donna.

"Then Uncle Scrooge ran off to Brazil to try to find Belle and failed miserably, and when he came back, Fan took me to meet him in his new office. He'd set up his own business and cut Scorpius out of his life."

"And they never spoke again?" she asked.

"No," said Fred, nursing his grog. "Uncle Eb never really got over the shock of Belle leaving – we were all shocked – but it broke him and he was a changed man when he came back. Of that I have no doubt."

"In what way changed?"

"He would never trust anyone ever again. I guess that's when he fell in love with money. I heard him tell Fan that at least money would never betray him." Fred looked at his wife. "Sad really," he added, squeezing his wife's hand.

Donna shook her head. "Nothing excuses his cruelty," she said, her mouth tight. "Nothing!"

"Perhaps, but I do feel for him and that is why I go every year and ask him to join us but the answer is always the same." Fred fell thoughtful for a moment before adding, "Maybe one year he will change his mind and come visit us."

"You believe that, Fred?"

Fred considered this for a long moment, looking deep into his pewter mug as he swilled around the dregs of his grog.

And as he did so, the Ghost looked at Old Scrooge and said, "Is it thumbs up or thumbs down, Scrooge?" Scrooge shrugged unhappily and returned his gaze to Fred, who had finally looked up from the inside of his pewter mug. "You know what, dear, I believe that one day Uncle Scrooge will come visit us."

His wife reached over and enfolded her husband in her ample bosom. "That's why I love you, Fred."

They kissed and Fred raised his pewter mug in the air. "To Uncle Scrooge!"

Slowly and reluctantly, Donna joined him. "To Uncle Scrooge." And a tear appeared in Old Scrooge's eye.

The scene slowly faded from view as the Ghost said, "See, Scrooge – someone does love you." And Scrooge spent a long moment looking at the spot where his nephew had disappeared. More tears formed.

"I did him wrong, Ghost," he said finally.

"You did indeed, Scrooge," said the Ghost, "but at least you know it, so that's a start." She turned to leave. "Come on, we've a lot more 'wronged' people to see. We've a busy night ahead of us!" And this time Scrooge did not get a mighty slap on the back.

50

As they travelled on the Vespa, the Ghost turned to look at Scrooge with her ever-changing eyes. "About this being your last year here on Earth, Scrooge. How would you feel about that?"

Scrooge's brow knitted and he shook his head violently. "That wouldn't give me enough time."

"For what?"

"You'd only laugh."

"Try me."

"Okay," said Scrooge with resignation. "I'm attempting to become the Richest Man on Earth." At this, the Ghost went into a paroxysm of laughter so great that she almost lost control of the Vespa. Scrooge regarded the Ghost coldly. "I really can't see what's so funny."

"Have you forgotten what your ghostly father warned you about?"

"Him?" Scrooge said bitterly.

"Yes, him," said the Ghost. "The man who risked everything to come back to save you!"

"I don't take anything he says seriously."

"Really?" said the Ghost. "You need to!"

And as they came to the House of Commons and crossed Westminster Bridge, the Ghost braked hard, almost throwing Scrooge onto the icy road.

"What are you doing?" Scrooge snapped as the Ghost dismounted, taking off her helmet and shaking out her orange locks of hair.

"Take a look around you, Ebby," she said. It was the first time she had used his familiar nickname, and Scrooge looked at her closely as he lifted a stiff leg over the scooter and stood shakily on his feet. The Ghost had proceeded over to the bridge's parapet and was gazing out at the River Thames and the city beyond. It had just begun to snow.

"Why are we stopped?" Scrooge asked.

"What do you see, Ebby?"

Scrooge looked at the vast expanse of buildings, apartment and office blocks, and the old historical sites that made up the heart of London. "Some good residential prospects."

"That's all?" the Ghost said, outraged. "I mean, that's all you really see?"

Scrooge scanned the horizon again. "Yes, good potential, if you picked the right areas of course."

"Potential for what?" The Ghost sounded exasperated.

"Potential to make money of course," Scrooge snapped.

"You're missing everything, Ebenezer Scrooge." The Ghost looked at Scrooge shaking her head. "There's only one thing for it."

And with that, she blew into the air above his head and made a scattering movement with her right arm. Scrooge watched, spellbound, as spots of gold light, no bigger than small daisy petals, appeared in the air and began falling, some settling on Scrooge's head, some on his shoulders. As they did so, Scrooge felt a tingling on his scalp, forehead, and arms; a sensation that made him let out a giddy laugh. And the giddy sensation passed down his throat and into his veins and soon his heart was thumping in his chest.

"What is this?" he cried out.

"Ha-ha, you don't know, Scrooge?"

"No."

"How does it feel?"

"I don't know," said Scrooge. "It feels alive, I guess. What is it?" Scrooge pointed a quivering finger at the remaining petals of light.

"That, Ebenezer Scrooge, is the spirit of Christmas."

Scrooge found himself giggling, as if he had been tipsy.

"The spirit of Christmas?" Scrooge laughed dismissively.

"Yes, it's what you are feeling now," the Ghost said. "Joy, laughter, and love."

And as Scrooge looked around, it was as if the scales had fallen from his eyes. His senses heightened and he heard muffled footsteps in the snow behind him, and turning, saw a young couple who were holding hands walking towards him. And Scrooge could see a halo of bright light surrounding them. He stood on the pavement directly in front of them and such was his wonder that he could not move. And the couple walked straight through him. And as they did so, he felt a pulse of warmth, of deep, unspoken feelings that made tears spring to his eyes. The couple paused and kissed just in front of him; a long, passionate kiss. And Scrooge felt a jolt of energy as petals of light emanated from their lips and suddenly, he felt a lump in his own throat.

"When did you last feel love, Ebenezer?" The Ghost whispered and there was a tenderness in the voice that had not been there before.

"I don't know," Scrooge said, brushing tears angrily away with his sleeve. The lovers began receding but still Scrooge could feel the warmth of their connection. See the halo of golden light that radiated from the hands that held each other tight.

The Ghost approached and said gently, "Everyone needs to be loved, Ebenezer." And for a long while Scrooge stood still on the bridge watching as the lovers faded from view, sensing that his mind had been opened up to possibilities that he had forgotten existed: the warmth that he had felt as they walked by, the thrill of their holding hands, the miracle of the kiss. And at this thought, there came unbidden the memory of his first kiss. And the memory made his every sense dizzy. He could feel again the softness of Belle's lips as they touched his. The warmth of her hand. The sweetness of her breath. The heat of her body. And for a long moment, Scrooge was overcome as he saw the look in Belle's eyes as she whispered, "I love you."

And it was as if a great curtain had been lifted and Scrooge could see again a life without bitterness or shadows, a life filled with love. The love of Belle. The promise of a future filled with light. Filled with hope – as it had been before the shadow fell.

51

"She loves you," the Ghost said simply, her eyes filled with a warm light.

"Who?"

"Belle!"

"No!" Scrooge murmured, feeling a sharp stab of pain in his chest at the mention of Belle's name. And the pain grew until it took over his whole being and the strength in his legs failed and he staggered so the Ghost had to hold him up. A deep sob came up from his very core, causing the Ghost to look at him with a sudden keenness.

"What is it, Scrooge?"

But Scrooge could not speak and waved the Ghost away. He shuffled over to the very edge of the bridge and, leaning with his hands on the parapet, he looked out across the Thames. St Paul's Cathedral stood illuminated by light but Scrooge's eyes did not rest on that. Instead, they zigzagged across the Millennium Bridge and over to the Tate Modern, before looking into the far distance, to Greenwich and beyond. And Scrooge took in a deep, desperate breath. Once. Twice. Before words formed on his thin, cracked lips.

"I can't feel—" he began but words failed him again. The Ghost moved closer, listening. Again, Scrooge took a deep breath, like a child recovering after a fit of crying. And all the time the snow fell, covering Scrooge in a fine film of silver crystals that glinted under the streetlights of Westminster Bridge.

"What is it, Ebenezer?" the Ghost repeated softly. And Scrooge glanced sideways at her, his eyes red-rimmed.

"I don't want to feel this…" he said.

The Ghost looked at him closely. "Feel what?"

"Love." And Scrooge looked to the Ghost so helpless that she laid a hand on him.

"You feel love again – yes?" the Ghost asked. Scrooge nodded.

"Belle's love?"

"Yes…" His face contorted in pain. "But how can I feel love for the woman who betrayed me?"

"Are you sure of that, Ebenezer?"

"Of what?"

"That she betrayed you?"

Scrooge looked surprised at the question. "What else am I to believe?"

"Believe what she told you the night before you were to be married," the Ghost said gently, but Scrooge shook his head angrily and turned away. The Ghost, with a gentle hand, brought him back to face her. "Remember that love, Ebby – feel it!"

Scrooge closed his eyes tight and his brow knitted in concentration. But after a moment, he opened them again, his eyes wild with distress. "I'm sorry, but I cannot feel anything except anger."

The Ghost looked at Scrooge with tenderness and touched the top of his head just once. And a single petal of light filled the air before settling on Scrooge. And in that moment, Scrooge felt himself transported back to his old house and the bedroom the night before their wedding, just as Belle placed a hand on her young lover's cheek. But this time Scrooge was no longer an onlooker; he *was* his younger self and he felt the warm touch of Belle and smelt the heady bouquet of her perfume… Scrooge let out a cry of alarm but again felt the Ghost's hand on his arm. "Steady now, Ebenezer." And this time Scrooge surrendered to his memory.

52

"I place my life in your hands, Ebenezer." It was the voice of Belle and Scrooge felt the miracle of being back with her and he clasped her hand desperately in his. It was warm and she squeezed back before her lips opened and she spoke to him. "And know this: I will always be yours, whatever happens. You understand?"

And Scrooge found himself uttering the same words he had spoken to her that night. For they were, after all, his words.

"'Whatever happens?' What do you mean?"

And Belle gave him a look that was a mixture of sadness and hope. "Just know I would never betray you. Whatever happens, know that."

Scrooge again searched Belle's eyes, and felt his doubt being replaced by a feeling of pure longing. Taking Belle's face in both his hands, he kissed her with a passion that he had never experienced before. He felt her resist, gently trying to prise herself from his lover's embrace. And then, realising something unseen and unspoken had happened, she returned his kisses with a passion that exceeded even his. They sank onto the bed in an embrace that signalled that they had both accepted that they were husband and wife, forming one body and one soul.

And Scrooge awoke from the memory with a start on Westminster Bridge as the snow fell and the realisation dawned.

"The baby is mine," he said, his eyes filled with a wild wonder. "The baby is mine!" he repeated, looking at the Ghost who nodded. "Is it alive?" Scrooge asked.

The eyes of the Ghost coalesced into a deep red, and again a nod.

"Your child is alive for now. But be warned, I cannot see your future, only what is true today."

Scrooge looked up at the stars. "I have a child," he said, his voice growing in wonder. "I have a child."

Scrooge's face was shining with a pulsing light and his eyes looked back at the Ghost with unaccustomed joy. But even as he looked, a shadow of doubt fell. "But?" he said, his voice wavering.

"But what, Scrooge?" the Ghost asked.

"Why did she keep this from me?"

The Ghost held Scrooge in her gaze. "Have you forgotten already?"

"Forgotten what?"

"Her begging you never to doubt her?"

"All I know is that she kept the existence of my child from me. What kind of woman does that?" And the old anger was now possessing him again. "Was it not enough to leave me standing on the altar like a fool?" he raged. "But to keep my child secret from me…" – he turned on the Ghost – "who would do that?"

The Ghost shook her head sadly. "Scrooge. Do you not see?"

"I see that I was betrayed first as a bridegroom and then as a father."

"Have you learned nothing, Scrooge?"

Scrooge's eyes were now filled with their old malice. "Oh yes! I've learnt that only fools trust people."

The Ghost shook her head. "I've no time for this nonsense," she said, walking back towards the scooter. "Come on."

"Come on where?"

"You'll find out soon enough." She slung her leg over the Vespa and gunned the engine, and he followed her reluctantly and they sped off into the snow.

53

Across the slumbering city of London, in a workman's hut on a piece of wasteland, the rat reappeared. It had been drawn out this time not by hunger, but something else. An instinct that made it look around the hovel. Suddenly its whole body stiffened and, letting out a high-pitched squeal, it sprang in one movement onto the inert shape that lay on the floor. It had seen another rat, brown and large, its massive yellow incisors preparing to take a bite out of the blue orbs that still gazed unknowingly at the ceiling. The black rat caught the intruder full on its side, sending it slip-sliding to the floor. The brown rat let out a sharp cry of alarm and was soon fighting back. But the bold attacker seemed possessed, sinking its teeth into the fur on the back of the brown rat's neck. But in return, it received a vicious scratch with a sharpened claw that raked its right eye and left it simpering in pain. Even then, half blind and crazed with pain, it still attacked until the brown rat turned and fled under the door and back into the snow outside.

The black rat turned and limping back, took up position on the body of the great, sleeping giant. And there it stayed, occasionally licking its ruined eye but nevertheless mounting what looked like guard, its head turning to face down the slightest threat, its teeth bared. And occasionally it looked up at the small rent in the ceiling, beyond which the shard of light could be seen beaming down.

The injured rat stayed in that alert position until night descended and the sound of Christmas carols filled the air nearby, along with the strumming of a slightly out-of-key guitar. The rat glanced up at the light above with its one good eye and, as if moved by an invisible force, left its place on the sleeping giant's chest, and came up to the place where the prone creature's breath smoked the air. The rat gently nudged the beard till the man stirred and woke. And in that instant, the rat limped off the stirring figure, taking shelter by the door, its one good eye never leaving the giant that slowly gathered itself. Finally, as the singing of Christmas carols swelled outside, the giant staggered upright and left the hut. And the rat, its job done, returned to its place of shelter to lick its wounds.

54

The Ghost took Scrooge around the back streets of London, following the course of the River Thames that appeared from time to time on their left, its surface glistening like a jewel. Finally, the scooter arrived at an open expanse of derelict ground, located between the twin office blocks where Scrooge's office stood.

An old oil drum had been placed right in the heart of the wasteland and it was belching clouds of black smoke and darting orange flames as it performed its job as a communal heater on this bitterest of Christmas Eve nights. And flames danced in the stiff wind, attracting the wasteland's strange inhabitants like moths.

The Ghost parked her Vespa by the side of a dirt track that the lorries and the diggers used. "Come on," she said, trudging across the open ground.

Scrooge followed reluctantly behind. The bombshell news that he was a father had been overshadowed by the greater betrayal of Belle. "She kept it from me," he kept repeating. "She kept it from me." Until a not-too-gentle slap on the back reduced him to silence.

Scrooge picked his way through the barren, snow-covered ground. He could make out a gathering of shapes. Outlines thrown up by the dancing flames. As he got closer, he could see that these strange shapes were actually people. People dressed in rags. People who wore black plastic refuse bags for protection against the cold. People who wore no shoes, despite the horrendous conditions, their feet black, bloodied, and ingrained with dirt.

"Here you will see the true spirit of Christmas!" the Ghost said as she pointed at the ragged band of homeless people.

"Here?" Scrooge said, his face twisted with distaste. The Ghost nodded.

"Yes, Scrooge, here!"

"Really?" Scrooge said in disbelief. A woman's voice he immediately recognised filled the air and Scrooge turned to discover the figure of Doctor Ellie standing in the midst of the homeless. She had a red Santa hat on the top of her mountainous pile of frizzled, snow-covered hair as she addressed the gathering. "Gather round, people," she began as Scrooge whispered urgently to the Ghost.

"I ran that woman out of my office yesterday!" he said, his lip curling in contempt.

"Why?" the Ghost asked.

"She was asking for money."

"For whom?"

Scrooge's eyes flicked around the collection of homeless souls. "This lot I suppose."

"Oh really?" said the Ghost, looking intently at Scrooge. "Listen to this woman, Scrooge, you may learn something!"

"I heard enough of her yesterday!" Scrooge said, but a look from the Ghost silenced him and he stood reluctantly and watched as Doctor Ellie stood addressing the small crowd. She stood behind a trestle table on which were two large thermos flasks. One was labelled TEA and the other COFFEE, while trays of sandwiches and plates of biscuits occupied the rest of the space. Behind Doctor Ellie was the dark outline of a battered van with the fading stencilled logo HELP THE HOMELESS.

A volunteer in a yellow bib manned a smaller trestle table laden with stacks of warm clothing and small toilet bags. While another volunteer came up beside Doctor Ellie with a 6-string guitar slung over her shoulder.

"Let's welcome Amy!" she said, beaming as the woman took the guitar in hand and began strumming notes. A few of the onlookers looked on curiously but none clapped. "Now listen up, everyone, that's not good enough!" Doctor Ellie continued, "Once we finish 'Silent Night' we have a special treat for you. But only if we all join in!" The good doctor beamed at the smattering of people as the guitarist strummed the opening chords of Silent Night as the impromptu carol service began.

At first, it was still only Doctor Ellie and her two helpers who sang. But with the doctor conducting furiously, the assortment of the homeless people began to mouth the words. They included an old woman in rags, whose mouth, Scrooge noted with distaste, was entirely devoid of teeth. She was joined by a Jamaican with dreadlocks and dressed in a full-length military great coat, performing some kind of disjointed dance.

A young girl, in particular, caught Scrooge's attention. She was, he guessed, barely out of her teens, yet she wore only a thin vest in the arctic cold, revealing skeletal arms covered in tattoos and riddled with needle marks. And so it went on. Finally, Scrooge turned to the Ghost. "Where is the spirit of Christmas?"

"You don't see it?"

"I only see misery."

"You're looking at it the wrong way, Scrooge."

"What's the right way?"

"You've already tried it. Go on," the Ghost said, "look with your new eyes and open your heart. You did it on the bridge with my help, now do it here on your own!" And the Ghost gave Scrooge an enormous clap on the back that jangled every last nerve in his body. "You can do it, Ebenezer!"

And Ebenezer Scrooge, with these words of encouragement ringing in his ears, began to look again for the true spirit of Christmas in this collection of misfits. At first he could only see the same mad, demented people dancing before him, but gradually something truly magical happened.

55

The vagrants' ruined bodies and rags were still visible to Scrooge's eyes but slowly a faint outline of light surrounded each individual. It was as if a shimmering energy was bursting out of each and every one of them.

"What's happening," Scrooge whispered. He glanced down at his hand and let out a cry. His fingers had acquired the same glowing energy field. "What is this?" he asked, holding up his hand.

"The force of life," the Ghost said. "The force that you bring into this life." And she moved her own shimmering hand through the air, a hand that glowed with the same energy. "This energy sustains you while you are here, Scrooge," she said, "and it continues after your death."

Scrooge could not take his eyes off his glowing hand. "But my father's hands were dark," Scrooge said.

"That was what he turned his light into during his life." The Ghost looked into Scrooge's eyes as if she was searching for something and suddenly her smile disappeared. "You would be shocked if you saw your true colours, Ebenezer Scrooge."

Scrooge did not seem happy to hear these words. "Why can't I see my true colours?" he demanded.

"You could if you tried, Ebenezer, but you are too caught up in your lies."

"What lies?"

"The lie that wealth is the only thing worth pursuing. The lie that everyone else is out to steal from you, including the likes of poor old George." The Ghost came closer to Scrooge till he had to shield his eyes from her gaze. "The lie that Belle betrayed you. But enough! I see that you are not yet ready to see the true spirit of Christmas so I will help you!"

56

The Ghost threw her hand over the gathering of people and petals of light filled the air and danced as they descended. And when Scrooge looked at the old woman, he let out a cry. All the horrors of age and neglect had disappeared to be replaced by what Scrooge could only describe as an unearthly beauty. It seemed the old woman's face shone with the majesty of her youth. She was glowing within with the same light that emanated from Scrooge's hand. "She is beautiful," he whispered in awe.

"She is indeed," said the Ghost, "but so is everyone else."

Scrooge looked at the other vagrants and let out a gasp as he saw the same transformation taking place. The Rastafarian was exuding a soft blue light, the beauty of which made Scrooge blink in disbelief. The old demented man was surrounded by an envelope of pure throbbing lime-green energy, and it seemed that his limbs were moving with a grace so mesmerising that Scrooge found it difficult taking his eyes off him. But it was the young girl who caught and held his attention. The heroin needle marks had vanished and shafts of pure white light extended from her back.

"Are they wings?" Scrooge mumbled as he turned to the Ghost.

"Now you see, Ebenezer," she chortled with delight. And bending near his ear, she whispered, "Angels walk amongst you unannounced."

"What?" said Scrooge, jolted out of his wonder. "I don't believe in angels."

And with that, the girl seemed aware of their stares, for she unfurled her wings that reached up to the heavens, spilling a curtain of light that slowly descended to the ground like spent fireworks.

"Just because you don't believe doesn't mean it doesn't exist!" the Ghost said and laughed uproariously. Then a voice caught Scrooge's attention and he turned to see Doctor Ellie. But it was not the Doctor Ellie he knew and loathed. Instead, her body radiated a warmth that he could feel, even from a distance. And as Doctor Ellie opened her mouth to speak, a torrent of gold particles appeared, flowing like water and bathing everyone around her.

Scrooge turned to the Ghost in wonder. "I see! I see!" he cried but instead of the jolly giant, Scrooge was blinded by the light of a thousand suns. And he fell to his knees in terrified awe as the Ghost spoke.

"We spirits are clothed so that you humans can bear our presence," the Ghost said. "Remember, I am the Spirit of Christmas, and I owe all my power to Him who came that first Christmas."

Scrooge was so overcome that he covered his ears and buried his head in the snow, fearing he would be consumed entirely by the light, as a strange and terrible terror took over his soul.

"Spirit – do not destroy me!"

The heat of the light seemed to recede and he felt the Ghost's hands touch his. And the touch was familiar. Scrooge squinted through a half-closed eye except the Ghost was no longer a burning supernova but the figure he knew, dressed in her gaudy Christmas jumper, her orange hair falling around her shoulders as she helped him up off the snowy ground.

"See, Scrooge," she said, pointing at the group gathered around the smoking, burning oil barrel. "We are all made of the same light. It's just that most refuse to see it."

And Scrooge looked up and saw the crowd of vagrants had resumed their former appearance: grubby, diseased, and dying. And Doctor Ellie reappeared dressed ridiculously as Santa Claus.

"More mince pies for everyone!" she cried, followed by a peel of her hearty laughter. The crowd moved forward and the pies disappeared in a twinkling as she began belting out "Feed the World" with her companion strumming the guitar while her daughter Tracy danced beside her.

"So that's the true spirit of Christmas," said Scrooge.

"Finally, Ebenezer Scrooge, I believe you understand!" the Ghost said approvingly. She raised her hand to give him a mighty clap on the back but at the sight of him tensing up, she changed her mind and laid it gently on his shoulder.

57

As Scrooge felt the Ghost's hand rest on his shoulder, he saw something that made his whole body tense. A tall, young man with long hair and a dirty poncho had threaded his way through the crowd and was talking urgently to Doctor Ellie. The young man's eyes were sunken deep into his skull and his whole body was trembling. "Good God," Scrooge said, as he turned to the Ghost, "that's the same man that came to my office yesterday."

Scrooge turned back to listen and found Doctor Ellie talking earnestly to the young man. "Okay," she said, taking out her mobile phone. "What's her number – her número?"

She dialled before handing the phone over. Scrooge noticed the young man's hand was trembling with the cold as he began speaking. He also noted that there were scars on the young man's wrists. "What are those?" he asked the Ghost but she motioned him to listen to the conversation.

"Mamãe," the young man said, tears filling his eyes. The tears turned into fits of coughing that wracked his whole body as he continued to speak. "Mãe – não venha eu vou ficar bem eu te amo!"

"What is he saying?" Scrooge asked the Ghost.

"He's telling his mother not to come," the Ghost whispered into Scrooge's ear. "He is telling her that he loves her."

Scrooge watched as the young man handed the phone back to the doctor, his face a mask of suffering. And as Scrooge looked, it was as if he saw him for the first time. The rat-like figure of the day before had transformed into a very real and very sick person.

"I don't know why this man's life should concern me," he said to the Ghost, "but it does."

They watched as the young man turned and left, despite Dr Ellie's protests. "Stay with us – we'll help you! Nós vamos ajudá-lo!" she exclaimed, following him and laying a restraining hand on his shoulder. He stopped and deliberately but gently removed it.

"I must go – eu tenho que ir," he said before a coughing fit took over. Doctor Ellie stood back reluctantly and allowed him to make his way towards Scrooge Towers, his head bent against the snow that began to fall heavily again. He staggered and fell as he went, drawing a cry from the doctor, but somehow he got back up on his feet and lurched forward until he was lost in the blizzard.

"Ghost," said Scrooge, looking into the wall of whiteness, "will he live?"

The Ghost shook her head. "His time on this Earth is very short."

"No!" Scrooge said. And in that moment, Scrooge's mind was clear. "We must help him," he said, turning to the Ghost.

There was a distant chime of a clock and the Ghost's hand tightened its grip on his shoulder. "You are right, Ebenezer, and we must hurry," she said, leading him back towards the scooter.

"Why the hurry?" asked Scrooge. She paused and turned. "Christmas Day is almost finished and with it my time here. We have only minutes to save him!"

58

The young man Jesu had become a vessel filled entirely with pain. Every jarring step that he took over the broken wasteland caused every nerve in his body to explode in agony. He was also shaking uncontrollably and his vision was blurring. The only thing that kept him going was the hazy dot of light that had suddenly appeared in the sky above him while he was talking to Doctor Ellie. And when he had seen it, he had immediately turned to follow. But soon his energy failed and he slipped on a rocky outcrop, and the ground came up to meet his face. Jesu heard a sharp crack echo in his skull and felt a stab of liquid fire in his mouth. He opened his eyes to see the snow turn red under his face. Tentatively, he reached up his fingers to feel the bloody mess of his cut lip and feel the rough surface where his front tooth had broken off. He spat out a mouthful of blood and fragments of shattered tooth and felt something snap inside. Nothing physical; it was much worse than that. The will to go on was all but broken. A deep sob came up through his throat, and a bloody cry rent the air. And in that moment, the young man Jesu prepared to give up his fight for life. As the young man's eyes closed over and he buried his head in the blood-soaked snow, a voice, he was sure it came from the shard of light, called him back.

GET UP, JESU! FOLLOW THE LIGHT!

It was the urgency of the words that roused him from his deadly stupor. Gritting what was left of his teeth, Jesu placed both the palms of his hands into the snow and pushed hard. But the jolt of pain in his head at the movement forced him to stop. With a great effort of will, he forced his eyes to look up and he saw the light again. It had descended and hovered in front of him. And with the light came an urgent call that he suddenly knew he must follow, and fast, before it was too late. Standing uncertainly on his feet, he began half-walking, half-running, his eyes only focused on the light that glowed softly in front of him, as it led him on towards the River Thames.

59

The Ghost and Scrooge roared off on the Vespa. They bumped and skidded over the wasteland and soon they had reached the back of Scrooge's building. The distant bells of St Paul's were chiming and Scrooge felt the air cackle with a sudden urgency.

"Come!" the Ghost said, heading off towards the river. Scrooge followed with a feeling that something very bad was about to happen.

60

Jesu reached the end of the wasteland and stopped dead in his tracks. The physical pain that had consumed his body was replaced by another: dread, as he looked at the building that the light was leading him towards. His palms were suddenly sweaty and he felt cold on his scalp where his hair stood on end. For the light was leading him directly to a place he would never choose to revisit – the place where he had been attacked and nearly drowned. And Jesu swayed on the spot, caught suddenly by the nightmare of indecision. To go back was not an option. He would soon die in the frozen wasteland. But to go forward to the very place where, just hours before, he had nearly lost his life? Every part of his broken body rebelled.

Jesu looked at the light that vibrated in the air just before him and inwardly pleaded with it to take him somewhere else, anywhere but here where the dark threatening waters of the River Thames flowed. The very waters in which he had so nearly lost his life. Black dots were suddenly dancing in front of Jesu's eyes. He blinked, reaching out an arm for support that was not there. His heart was thumping so hard in his chest that he thought it would explode. He closed his eyes and silently implored the light for help. Nothing happened. No answering call. And when he opened his eyes again, the light had disappeared and he was left entirely alone with only terror as his companion.

61

Scrooge and the Ghost turned the corner of his building and saw Jesu standing in front of Scrooge Towers, swaying on his feet and looking as if he was about to collapse. "He needs help," Scrooge said, starting forward but the Ghost lay a restraining hand on him as the sliding doors of Scrooge's palatial office opened and Bobbi Cratchit and her son Tim ran straight towards Jesu, just as he collapsed to the ground.

62

"Grab him, Tim," said Bobbi, catching Jesu under the arm.

Tim was supporting the other arm and though he was just seven years old, he did so with ease; for Jesu's body was skeleton thin and it felt to Tim like he weighed less than the clothes he stood in. They found a seat by the river and Bobbi knelt down in front of Jesu and held both of his hands in hers. She had to fight down the urge to cry out at the state he was in: the red-rimmed eyes, the hollowed-out cheeks, and the caked blood and stumps of broken teeth. But even before Bobbi called for help, she knew there was one thing she must do.

"Is this yours, Jesu?" she said, fishing the silver locket out of her pocket.

His bloodshot eyes widened and his whole body quivered as he whispered, "Obrigado, Bobbi – onde você o encontrou – where did you find it?"

"Down by the river," she answered. Tears of joy welled in his eyes.

"Você não sabe o que isso significa para mim – you don't know how important this is. Obrigado, obrigado!" Two tears ran down his face and Bobbi clasped him to her, but tenderly, as she felt the arms of her son wrap around them both.

"Obrigado, obrigado – thank you, thank you!" Jesu continued, but suddenly his eyes opened wide in alarm and he pulled roughly back from the embrace.

"Vá embora, Bobbi, leave!" he said. He went to stand, but Bobbi's hand pushed him back down.

"We're not going anywhere. I'm calling an ambulance."

"Você não entende!" Jesu said, pushing himself up, his sudden strength belying the wretched state he was in. "Leave, now!"

63

"Ghost, what is wrong?" Scrooge said. They were standing in front of the building, looking at the unfolding scene. The Ghost did not answer and Scrooge followed her gaze. Striding purposefully along the quayside was a group of four youths. Two were wearing black bomber jackets, one a long black Crombie coat, while the fourth wore only a T-shirt, the sleeves cut short, revealing muscles covered in tattoos. One tattoo immediately caught Scrooge's eye: ENGLAND 4 THE ENGLISH, with a swastika bookending the black inked words. The bells of St. Paul began chiming and everything momentarily slowed down.

"Who are they?" Scrooge asked, as the four men approached.

"These are your children, Scrooge, the fruit of your actions."

"What are you talking about—" But Scrooge's complaint was cut short by a harsh shout.

"Oi!" It was the youth with the T-shirt who had reached the bench and began circling it like a lion. "Is this the lad you pushed in the river?" he said, glancing at the man in the Crombie coat.

"Yeah, that's him alright!"

Bobbi Cratchit stood as the youths surrounded them, not letting go of Jesu's hands.

"Leave him alone!" she said.

"Mum?" Tim cried out in fear as he clung to his mother.

"It's okay, dear," she said, placing his tiny hand in Jesu's as she turned to face the four.

"Bobbi, por favor vá! Go!" said Jesu, trying to stand but swaying back and collapsing on the seat. A fierce wind swept across the river, buffeting those standing on the quay, sending the black Crombie coattails flapping as snow stung the eyes. There was a distant boom as the bells chimed out. The man in the Crombie peered down at Jesu.

"He don't look too good," he said, a grimace turning his face sour. "I've called the police," Bobbi said. "You'd better scarper — they know you nearly killed him the last time. They're looking out for you!"

There was a chorus of jeers. "Put him out of his misery, I'd say," the guy with the cut-off T-shirt said, moving ominously forward. There was a glittering flash and a steel blade appeared in his hand as if by magic, the razor-sharp stiletto point reflecting the light.

"Mum!" Tim let go of Jesu's hand and clung to his mother's arm.

"Grab 'em!" the man wielding the blade said.

64

"Ghost, we must help them!" Scrooge said, striding forward to confront the assailants. But his body merely passed through theirs, and Scrooge stood helpless, looking from the man wielding the blade back to the Ghost.

"It's too late," the Ghost said as the chimes heralding midnight rang out. "Your time for helping has passed, as has mine." She was beginning to collapse, to disintegrate into the ground before Scrooge's eyes.

"What's happening to you, Spirit?" Scrooge said, panic in his voice.

"My time here on Earth has ended. You are alone – I cannot help you anymore."

"Don't leave me!" said Scrooge, falling to his knees, but the Ghost was fast disappearing into thin air as the chimes rang out. Her orange hair had gone and her Christmas jumper was turning into dust. "What shall I do?" Scrooge implored her, shaking an arm that shattered and turned to smoke.

"I have shown you all I could," she said, as her face faded away, "Now it is up to you, Ebenezer Scrooge—" And with a gust of wind, she was gone.

Scrooge watched in disbelief and then turned to witness the unfolding action as Bobbi Cratchit and Tim wrestled with the men. But they were held by two of the youths while the man in the T-shirt approached Jesu.

"You had your warning, mate," he said, raising the blade, the swastika on his bicep bulging. The blade came up and down in a slow arc and plunged into the heart of Jesu. He let out a small gasp and looked at the man who held the blade. He fell to his knees and toppled back against the bench as the killers fled, laughing like hyenas.

And Ebenezer Scrooge stood feeling numb as the words of the Ghost echoed in his head:

These are your children, Scrooge. You have created them!

He had failed the Ghost of Christmas Present just as he had failed the young man. And then it hit him harder than all: he had failed his father. The father who had ventured through the valley of death to be with him and warn him of his peril. He had failed his father and must now suffer the dire consequences. And as he looked on the dying figure of Jesu, he saw the light of his young life being slowly extinguished. And in that moment, he felt Jesu desperately reaching out to him as if he had something important to say.

But as the final chime of midnight echoed in the air, the light in Jesu's eyes finally went out and blackness descended on Ebenezer Scrooge, who knew no more.

Part 4 –
The Ghost of Christmas Future

65

Scrooge was surrounded by a thick cloud of darkness as a dim light appeared in the distance, revealing a figure cloaked in black. As the figure approached, Scrooge could make out the many folds of its great black cloak and burning red eyes glimpsed behind the hood that was pulled forward, so its face was hidden. Scrooge felt fear but made himself stand tall as he addressed the spectral being.

"You must be the Ghost of Christmas Future, and I fear you more than any other spirit I have met. But I know we must journey together."

Scrooge swallowed hard as he caught the faint rasp of the Ghost's breathing, like echoes from a subterranean underworld. "Lead on!" Scrooge said, standing tall, his head finally clear. "The night is short, and we have much to do – lead on!"

The Ghost did not answer or show in any manner or way that he had understood what Scrooge had said. But a skeletal hand was lifted into the air, where it pointed at the threatening clouds.

Scrooge at first saw nothing, but soon the clouds parted and there, high above, was a flash of lightning and Scrooge held his breath as he saw that the flash was blood red. The bolt hit the ground with a mighty crack and a cloud of black, billowing smoke erupted, and then slowly but surely, a figure emerged.

66

"Scorpius!" Scrooge gasped.

The Ghost of his father had changed dramatically since Scrooge had last seen him. He seemed thinner, more stretched out, as if suffering had eroded his being to the point where he could barely exist. And when Scorpius spoke, his voice was suffused with agony. "Son, you have failed and should be condemned to wear the chains that you forged in life."

The ghost looked at Scrooge with horror, as if he could already see the chains in place and Scrooge shuddered inwardly. "But I have begged that you be given a second chance," the ghost continued, "and my prayer has been answered." Scorpius managed to raise his head and look at his son. "We must go, for my time for confessing to you has arrived." And reaching out a wizened hand, he offered it to Scrooge.

Scrooge looked at his father's eyes, dull orbs of sadness that made him feel a deep unease. "You are much changed, Father," he said. The eyes of his father regarded him for a long, unblinking moment.

"My crimes weigh heavier on me now that I have seen them enacted again." He paused while distant sobs and the sound of lost souls' lamentations filled the air. "But I have more horrors to show you. More crimes to confess."

Scrooge hesitated for just a moment before taking his father's hand. He was not sure how much more misery he could endure or how many more shocks. But he had no time to think further as, with a flash of dark light, they disappeared.

67

Scrooge could feel the pain that his father was suffering by merely gripping his hand. It was as if Scorpius was exposed to one long and continuous force of regret that contorted his soul.

"Father, you suffer so, what can I do to help?"

The dark light that surrounded him shimmered. "You are helping me, son," Scorpius said.

"How?"

"By listening to the lessons that you are shown and by changing your ways," he said, and it seemed to Scrooge that the ghost of his father felt no small satisfaction at this. "But come, we are nearly there."

And Scrooge noticed that they had arrived in a place that he recognised, though it had been long buried in his past.

"This is Belle's house?" he asked.

"Yes, this is the morning of your wedding," Scorpius announced, as they both looked at the scene unfolding before them.

A police car was parked by the curb outside and they watched as a younger Scorpius Scrooge nodded to the two police officers standing by the car and said the words: "Wait here."

Scorpius walked from the parked police car up to the door of the small terraced house, and Scrooge and the ghost followed. Scorpius was dressed in sombre black clothes and he had a sheaf of papers in his hand. He knocked hard on the door, which was opened by Belle. She was in her wedding dress but without the veil and carried a make-up brush in her hand.

Scrooge looked at the ghost, confused, "She's already emptied my bank account – shouldn't she be heading for the airport?"

"Shhh," said the ghost of Scorpius. "This is the moment you learn everything, my son."

But Scrooge was still perplexed. "Why is she dressed in her wedding gown? And what are the police doing here?" Scrooge slowly turned back to the ghost of his father. "What are you doing here, Father?"

And Scorpius gave his son such a look of dread that Ebenezer Scrooge steeled himself for the worst.

68

When Belle opened the door, her face fell. "What are you doing here?" she said, then noticing the two police officers behind him, her hand flew to her mouth. "Is Ebby okay?"

"He's fine," Scorpius said, thrusting the sheaf of papers into her hand. "Read these." His voice was terse and Belle took the papers and began reading them, and all the time the frown on her face deepened.

"What is this?" she said, holding up the documents.

Scorpius Scrooge shook his head sadly.

"These officers are here to arrest you, Belle, unless you do exactly what I say." The frown deepened on Belle's face.

"Arrest me? For what?"

"For stealing all my son's money. It's all there."

He stabbed at the documents that Belle was holding.

"This is ridiculous," she said, shoving the papers back. "I'm calling Ebenezer."

She turned to leave but Scorpius placed a hand on her shoulder. "You will be arrested the moment you try that." The two pig-eyes bore into Belle, and he leant forward and thrust the papers back at her. "The evidence shows you went to Ebenezer's bank and took all his money. Every last penny." The pig eyes seemed to stare right into Belle's soul. "The evidence is all here. You're a thief and a fraudster."

Belle recoiled. "You did this?" she said furiously, her hands suddenly shaking. He nodded, his face twisted into a malevolent grin.

"You can't get away with this—"

"Belle, Belle," he said like a teacher talking to a backward student, "I have already got away with it." He glanced at the two officers who were waiting, like dogs straining at the leash. "The police have been provided with details of your bank account in Brazil, as well as the plane ticket you booked for your flight to Brazil leaving at noon." He smiled again, glancing at his wristwatch. "Thought that was a nice touch, booking a flight at the exact time your husband is waiting at the altar."

"I'm phoning Eb," Belle said, turning away, but within her taking three steps, the police were at the doorway.

69

"Ms Belle Santiago, we're arresting you for theft."

Belle turned, her eyes imploring.

"I have done nothing!"

"You'll have plenty of time to explain all that to the judge," the police officer said. "Please come with us."

"So you are in on this!" Belle said, hysteria finally taking over, looking from the policeman back to Scorpius. "You bribed them?"

"A moment," Scorpius said to the police officer. He nodded and they returned to the car, leaving Scorpius and Belle alone. "Let me spell this out for you, Belle. If you don't do as I ask, you'll spend the next ten years locked away in a prison cell."

"Ebenezer won't allow that—"

Scorpius could not contain his laughter. "Ebenezer will be presented with irrefutable evidence that you stole all his money and planned to flee the country at the exact moment he was standing at the altar." He leant in to her. "Surely you know my son well enough to know how he will react to having all – and I mean ALL – his money stolen, let alone the humiliation of being stood up at the altar."

Belle let out a cry, like an animal that had been shot through the heart by a hunter's arrow and knows, in that instant, that the wound is fatal.

Scorpius smiled. "But it's not all bad. There is another way out," he said.

Tears pooled in Belle's eyes and spilled down her face. "I think I'm pregnant with your son's child."

Scorpius shrugged. "It doesn't matter."

"What do you mean it doesn't matter?"

"If you stay here and fight me, any child you have will be taken from you the moment it is born. And you will never win custody, never see your baby." Belle let out an involuntary sob. "But if you follow my instructions—"

"Why are you doing this to me?" she said, the tears freely running down her face. Scorpius's eyes narrowed.

"Because you defied me. Now will you do as I say?"

And the scene faded into darkness, leaving Scrooge facing the ghost of his father.

70

Ebenezer turned on his father. "Why did you do this?"

"Why?" the ghost repeated, shaking his head. He looked shrunken and defeated. "I have asked that question a thousand times and still I am not sure of the answer." The ghost sighed and seemed lost in dark thoughts. "My pride," he said finally, "would not allow a woman of low birth and colour to take you from me."

"That's a lie!" Scrooge shouted. "You *never* wanted me from the moment I was born. Why did you ruin everything I had with Belle?"

"Yes, yes! You are right," the ghost agreed. "I never wanted you after Barbara died but I didn't want you to be happy with anyone else after all you had done to me."

"I was a baby!"

"I know, I know," said Scorpius, his face ravaged by grief. "I was wrong and it filled me with remorse. I followed Belle to Rio to make sure she did not contact you."

"To Rio, why?"

"I was suddenly filled with terror about what you would do if you ever found out. Here, you must see for yourself."

The scene changed and from the darkness emerged the younger Scorpius in the riot of colour that was Rio, and Scrooge watched his father follow Belle from a distance. And Scrooge's face warped in bitterness as he saw a dark, handsome man at Belle's side as she carried her baby back to the favela.

Suddenly Scrooge let out a cry, as, out of the crowded streets, came the figure of his younger self, his face gaunt as he looked around the square where Belle lived, just missing Belle as she nursed baby Jesu on the balcony.

"You saw me?" Scrooge asked. And the ghost nodded to his son, his eyes filled with regret. "I saw you, and at that moment, I understood what I had done."

"Why didn't you come after me?" asked Scrooge.

"I did, but you were swallowed up by the crowds."

"And in London? You could have contacted me when you got back."

"Yes, son, but within days of returning, I feel ill. My betrayal eating me up. I knew I must confess and I got Fan to call you from the hospital…" His voice petered out.

"And I did not come," said Scrooge.

The scene changed to Scorpius's hospital with him gasping on his deathbed as a dark shadow entered the room and fell across him.

"I was going to confess all to Fan when she returned," the ghost of Scorpius sobbed. "But Death took me and my soul has been in torment ever since."

"Why didn't Belle come looking for me after your death?" said Scrooge. "You had no hold on her."

"I had told her in Rio that no matter what happened to me, the police would arrest her the moment she landed in London, and she would never get back to see her child again." There was a long pause as the ghost sighed with regret. "She would never leave her child, even though she loved you."

Scrooge looked at the ghost of his father with disbelief. "Belle never loved me."

"Not only did she love you, Ebenezer, she still does."

The scene changed back to Scrooge in his penthouse office surveying the world, his face a mask of bitterness. And beside him, unseen, the Ghost of his father looking on in agony.

"Once I died, I had to watch as the consequences of my actions played out," the ghost of Scorpius continued. "See you, without the love of Belle, turn into the heartless creature you are today. See Belle watch her child grow without ever knowing their true father. Watch them try to search for you."

"Search for me?"

"Oh yes, do you not yet understand? That young child of yours fell apart looking for you. You were the hole in his heart he could not fill." Scrooge remembered the scars on Jesu's wrists.

"He tried to kill himself…"

"Yes," the Ghost said, "And I had to watch all this. The attempts on his life, the drugs he used to dull his pain, and all because of the lie that I had created. The lie that Belle had stolen all your money." And tears of a dark hue flowed down the ghost's ruined face. "And I had to watch you as the lie ate away at your soul like cancer. Knowing you, my one and only son, could have had true happiness with Belle by your side, and your child in your arms."

Scrooge looked at his father and even as he did, he knew he had a monumental choice to make: to forgive his father or punish him. For a moment, the two choices wrestled in his conscience. But the well-worn pathways of bitterness and hatred won out in the end.

"You destroyed my future!" Scrooge said, turning on his father. "You destroyed all our futures."

The ghost of Scorpius fell to his knees and, with outstretched hands, begged, "Forgive me, son, forgive me."

Scrooge briefly saw a flash of light in the gathering darkness and for a long moment he looked at his father, begging on his knees directly in front of him. He took a breath, trying to keep that one spark of light alive, but the feeling of disgust for the kneeling figure won out and the mote of light was extinguished: "Never! I will NEVER FORGIVE YOU!"

The ghost closed his eyes on hearing his son's rebuttal and luminous tears flowed from his eyes.

"Then we are all lost and the darkness takes over!" And with that, he disappeared into the tunnel of darkness, leaving his son alone with the forbidding presence of the Ghost of Christmas Future, who raised a skeletal hand and pointed it directly at Scrooge.

71

There was a great crash of thunder, and suddenly Scrooge found himself in the graveyard beside his home. He was standing under the great statue of the angel that protected the graves of his mother Barbara and his hated father Scorpius. A cortege was making its way up towards the grave where Ebenezer Scrooge stood. At the front was a coffin being carried by six pallbearers all in black. Bobbi and Tim followed, with Fred and his family behind. Doctor Ellie and a tall couple took up the rear.

Scrooge looked hard at the coffin. "This is my funeral?" he asked the dark and forbidding Ghost who stood by his side, but no answer came.

Scrooge looked at the last two mourners as they approached. The tall woman on the right wore a black mantilla that covered her face. The man to her left had a black homburg hat pulled down tight against the driving snow, and his features were hidden.

"Who are they?" he asked the Ghost of the Future but again no answer.

The coffin was lowered beside the freshly dug grave and Scrooge watched closely as the lady in the mantilla came forward. She was carrying a single red rose and motioned to one of the pallbearers to remove the coffin lid.

"Why were they mourning my death?" Scrooge asked the Ghost, shaking his head. "They all hated me." He moved closer to the woman just as a gust of wind lifted her mantilla and revealed her face.

72

"Belle!"

Scrooge felt his heart ready to burst. "Why is she here?" he asked the Ghost but still no answer came. Scrooge fell to the ground before her, reaching out his hands in supplication. "Dearest Belle, I'm so sorry for not trusting you." But she could not hear him and instead knelt by the coffin as the lid was removed. "Belle, look at me!" Scrooge continued, trying with every fibre and sinew to reach out to her. The Ghost raised his hand and pointed at the clock tower and Scrooge knew he had no time left.

"Belle, I love you!" he said, reaching out to her with trembling hands. "Don't grieve for me – I am not worthy."

The coffin lid was pulled back, and Belle flung herself forward, but not onto the body of Ebenezer Scrooge. And Scrooge looked on in disbelief at the corpse being enfolded in Belle's arms.

"No!" he said. "It cannot be," he continued as he looked into the pale face of the young man Jesu.

73

Scrooge stood stunned as he saw Jesu's body wrapped in the arms of his love, Belle, as her tall companion leaned down to comfort her.

"Irmã, por favor," he said, drawing Belle to him but she shrugged him off. "Irmã, por favor," he said again, but she only shook her head as she held the inert body in her arms and motioned for him to stand aside.

Bobbi Cratchit came over and put a comforting arm around him.

"Julio, give your sister some time," she said.

It took a moment for the word to register in Scrooge's fevered mind. "Sister?" he said, looking at the young man. "He's her brother?" he shouted at the Ghost. And this time the Ghost did respond by raising a skeletal finger and pointing at the freshly placed gravestone that stood above the grave.

Scrooge turned towards the gravestone, his whole body trembling. It was covered in a thin layer of snow. There was a gust of wind as the storm broke, and slowly the name was revealed as a great wind raged around them. Scrooge fell to his knees in front of the Ghost. "Say this is not true!" he begged, but the Ghost of the Future only pointed his finger at the writing on the gravestone, now plain to see.

JESU SANTIAGO-SCROOGE

Scrooge looked at the body in the coffin, and it was as if the scales had fallen from his eyes. He saw the chiselled chin, the long aquiline nose, the sallow complexion, and the flop of hair. He looked up at the Ghost towering above him and bringing his hands together in supplication he cried out: "Ghost, I have learnt the lessons of my past, my present, and future and I HAVE CHANGED!" Then he raised his clasped hands towards the threatening spirit. "Let me wash away the writing on that stone. Let me save my son – save myself!"

There was a great crash of thunder as the ground beneath his feet gave way. He fell, grabbing hold of the coffin to stop his fall. And he came face-to-face with the dead body of Jesu, and suddenly Ebenezer Scrooge saw himself.

"What have I done to you, son?" he said, and with a great cry, he fell into the grave. And as he fell, he heard in the distance, far above, the voice of his father calling to him one last, desperate time: "Forgive me, Ebenezer, and you also shall be forgiven."

And with that, Ebenezer Scrooge was swallowed by the blackness and knew no more.

Part 5 –
Redemption

74

Ebenezer Scrooge fell for such a long time that he could not imagine any other sensation but falling into darkness. His body was nauseous with dizziness. His breathing came in such short breaths that he felt lightheaded. His skin felt a creeping chill, and his throat was parched. But it was his heart that bore the greatest burden. It thumped in his chest so hard and fast from grief and regret that it became the only sound he could hear. Scrooge opened his mouth to cry out, but instead of his voice, he heard only his heartbeat speeding up and growing louder until it obliterated all his other senses, leaving him gripped by a black terror. The beating drum reached a frantic crescendo until, with an explosion of energy, Scrooge found himself smashing into a solid surface. He squeezed his eyes shut but could still see light suddenly flooding through his eyelids. However, the landing had been soft, and the floor was not hard but a deep pile carpet. There was a familiar smell. He opened an eye just enough to squint out. Yes, the smell came from the carpet… and the carpet came from his room. His eyelids opened cautiously, doubting what his senses were telling him. The threads of the carpet were as familiar as the smell. He saw the wooden base of a sofa, and above it, the blue, soft leather he knew so well.

Tentatively, Scrooge pushed himself up on his hands. The leaded windows of his luxurious home glinted back at him as beams of sunshine filtered through. Scrooge pushed himself up until he was standing unsteadily on his feet.

"I'm alive?" It took him a second to realise it was his own voice echoing dully in the room. He paused, feeling the same palpitations as he feared the worst. Feared to see ghosts who would tell him what to do—feared to see his own father again in his agony. Except there was no one there but himself.

He was alive and entirely alone in his own front room.

75

"I'm alive," Scrooge said, and for the first time in a long, long time, his face broke into something unexpected: a smile. "I'm alive," he said again, this time as a statement. "I'm alive!" he shouted suddenly, jumping from one leg to the other. "I'm alive!"

And suddenly, it felt like his beating heart would explode not with terror but with something he thought he would never feel again: hope.

He ran over to the window and looked out. His eyes took in the bright shaft of sunlight shining through the pane of glass. A shaft of light so pure it seemed as if he were seeing the very photons and particles of light illuminating the sofa from which he had fallen. His eyes caressed the texture, his nose breathed in the familiar smell of the leather, and his ears took in the sound of the songbirds chirping outside. Scrooge placed a hand on his heart, feeling it pump in his chest, not from fear but from a newfound peace. Its beat steady, solid, quiet. The heartbeat of a man finally released from his ordeal. A tear appeared in the eye of Ebenezer Scrooge and this time he let it come.

"Thank you," he said as he approached the window, his eyes taking in the blue sky. "Thank you, spirits," he said softly and with reverence. His eyes caught the steeple of the church just as the peregrine falcon took off and circled the sky in great, exultant swoops. "Thank you," Scrooge said, softly like a prayer, blowing the great bird a kiss. He focused his eyes on the church and added, "I will not forget your lessons."

And in that moment, the church bell chimed, and Ebenezer Scrooge's eyes were suddenly filled with urgency. "Jesu!"

76

Scrooge threw open the window and looked out. A youth was passing on a scooter and, glancing up at the waving figure, braked to a halt.

"Hey, what day is it?" Scrooge asked, leaning out of the window.

"What?"

"What day is it, my fine fellow?"

The youth's spotty face twisted into a grimace. "You taking the mickey?"

Scrooge broke into a smile and shook his head. "No, certainly not! Wait there!" he said and he disappeared from the window. The youth went to restart his scooter and drive off when the door opened, and a tall figure loomed towards him down the snow-covered driveway.

"Blimey," the youth muttered, "a nutter!" For the approaching figure did indeed look strange. He had what looked like pyjamas on and was wearing red leather slippers on his bare feet. But it was the gaunt, unshaven face and mad, staring eyes that made the youth recoil as the figure stopped in front of him.

"I need a loan of your scooter!"

"What?" said the youth, fumbling to start the engine and get away.

"No, I'm serious," said Scrooge, taking several crisp new £100 notes out of his pocket and presenting them to the youth. "This is yours if you'll lend me your bike for the day! Go on, count them!"

"What's your game then?" the youth asked.

"I've a mission to complete. Now show me how to operate this" – Scrooge looked at the scooter grimacing – "fine machine."

The youth examined the notes again and finally satisfied he was not being scammed, put them in his pocket and dismounted the bike. Three minutes later, Ebenezer Scrooge was zig-zagging dangerously down the icy road while the youth looked on, shaking his head.

"And you'll need this helmet!" the youth shouted, running after the retreating figure. But Scrooge had disappeared from view. The youth fished into his pocket and took out the crisp, new notes, looking at them incredulously. "What a nutter," he said, as he began plodding down the snow-covered lane.

77

Ebenezer Scrooge twice nearly hit the curb and once narrowly avoided a traffic light positioned in the middle of the road, before he successfully reached the River Thames. Scrooge was faithfully following the youth's directions. "Keep the Thames on your left hand, mate, and you can't miss it." So far, so not very good. Sweat was pouring from Ebenezer Scrooge's brow, and his pyjamas were soaked. Only the thin overcoat offered any resistance to the biting cold, which had now entirely frozen Scrooge's body. But desperation drove him on, and a smile appeared on his face when he caught sight of his building, among the towering office blocks hugging the side of the Thames.

He did not see the police car stationed in a side road as he broke yet another red light, but he did hear the siren wailing behind him as it began its pursuit. Scrooge glanced back, a near-fatal mistake as the scooter wobbled and went into a side spin. "Spirits help!" he cried out, and somehow the bike righted itself, but the police car was gaining fast. If it caught him... But Scrooge dismissed the thought and opened the throttle instead. The scooter leaped forwards, but so did the police car.

"Pull in!" the PA system of the police car blared in Ebenezer Scrooge's ear. He was racing down the road hugging the Thames, but the 50cc engine was no match for the police Land Rover. Scrooge could hear the tires of his pursuers cutting through the thin crust of snow and knew that within seconds they would run him off the road. He looked up and immediately felt a flood of relief. The open wasteland where he had encountered Doctor Ellie was on his left. If he could only make the slip road, but even as he thought this, he felt a violent jolt from behind as the police Land Rover nudged him.

"Pull over!" a voice shouted. Scrooge clutched the scooter's handlebar while preparing for the inevitable crash. But with a sudden surge, the scooter regained balance and remained upright. The police Land Rover was now beside him, and a red-faced officer bellowed at him, "PULL OVER."

Scrooge saw the slip road open up on his left and, waiting until the very last second, he flung the scooter onto the icy side road. And whether due to Divine intervention or his growing skill, he skidded off the main road and up the slip road with barely a wobble. The scooter's engine was screaming, the needle in the red zone of the dial. Scrooge throttled back, gazing across at the building in whose shadow his son was taking refuge. But how to get over to him? The strip of wasteland between the slip road and his towering office block was filled with rocks and potholes, all covered in a thick layer of snow and ice.

There was another wail of the siren, and Scrooge glanced back, his brow a lather of sweat despite the freezing cold. The police Land Rover was behind him again and closing fast, its 4-wheel drive pushing it on towards his faltering scooter. It seemed that Scrooge had literally run out of road.

78

The police car was close behind, rolling and rollicking like a steamship on a storm-tossed ocean, and this made up Scrooge's mind for him. He yanked hard right and drove straight into the pristine, snow-covered wasteland. He clutched the two handles of the scooter, expecting at any second to be tipped over as he hit a rock or disappeared into a pothole. But somehow, the scooter held its course, juddering and jolting as the uneven terrain flung him this way and that, like a bucking bronco. Scrooge glanced back as he heard a frightening jolt of steel on rock and saw the Land Rover had crashed to a halt and was tilting on its side.

"What the..." Scrooge muttered. The police vehicle had followed in his exact tracks but had hit a rock he had not seen. "Thank you!" he whispered as he glanced up. Scrooge felt his mind clearing of panic and a great resolve filled him.

"I'm coming, son," he called out, steering the scooter in the direction of the buildings. He exited the wasteland and roared towards the back of his building. He did not see the two policemen exit their stranded vehicle and make their way after him on foot, shouting into their walkie-talkies as they went in pursuit.

79

"Leave him alone!" Bobbi Cratchit's words were cut off as one of the two thugs holding her clamped a hand over her mouth.

"Yeah, shut it!" said the man standing over the slumped figure of Jesu.

"Deixa eles irem," Jesu said. "Let them go."

The man in the T-shirt looked questioningly at Jesu. The muscles on his bare arms contracted, making the swastika tattoo swell, as he brought the stiletto blade up in the air. "Hold 'em," he said, as Tim and Bobbi struggled to get free. "I want them to see this."

Jesu looked from the man's eyes to the blade slowly rising above his head and suddenly, his eyes widened. For above the glinting blade was another light, brighter and clearer. And as his attacker prepared to strike, he saw something in Jesu's eyes that made him pause for the briefest of seconds. And in that moment, everything changed.

80

Ebenezer Scrooge gunned the scooter up the side of his building, hearing the distant chime of St Paul's. As the bells chimed, Scrooge was filled with certainty that he had only until the last chime to save his son. But even as that certainty possessed him, filling him with a deadly intent, the scooter motor sputtered and died, and the bike came to a shuddering halt. Scrooge stepped off stiffly and cast the machine aside. He began stumbling along the snow-covered runway in the shadow of his building, just as the great bell of St. Paul's chimed again.

"Spirits help me," he implored as he slip-sided along. He could see the waters of the Thames glittering in the noonday sun. But even as he forced his exhausted limbs forward, the chimes of midday continued to echo out. He slid, fell, slid again, and picked himself up. But he was still in the shadow of the building when the last chime rang out.

He exited onto the quayside just in time to see the glint of a knife in the distance. "No!" Scrooge cried as he flung himself towards the figure of his son standing upright before his attacker.

"Stop, you filth!" Scrooge cried as he came to a halt before the band of thugs. The man with the stiletto turned and a smile twisted his face at what he saw.

"Heh, it's the rich guy that owns that building!"

"Let them go," said Scrooge, regaining his breath and walking towards him with a purposefulness that made the man's face darken.

"I thought you were one of us?" he said.

"Not any more – let him go!" continued Scrooge as he approached within striking distance.

The man with the blade sneered: "You one of them now?"

Scrooge stood beside Bobbi and Tim. "Yes. I'm one of them."

The man raised the blade above his head. "You asked for it, mate."

He went to plunge the dagger into Scrooge, when two hands were flung around his neck, pulling him backwards and off balance. Jesu had launched himself from behind with the last ounce of his strength and this allowed Scrooge to reach up and grab the blade while Bobbi bit the hand of her captor, who released his hold with a cry of pain. Tim kicked the shin of his captor, who screamed out while the seven-year-old leapt to the defence of his mother. But the muscle-bound man in the T-shirt was powerful and had grasped Bobbi by the neck, bringing the sharp point of the stiletto down on her.

"No," Tim shouted, jumping at the attacker. But the man's strength was too great, and with a hideous animal growl, he threw off Scrooge and Tim, and pushing Bobbi aside, lunged at Jesu and the blade struck Jesu in his side. There was a scream and the assailant stepped back, his blade dripping with blood. But he had no time for triumph as Ebenezer Scrooge jumped him, knocking him to the ground and sending the blade clattering across the icy pavement. "Not so brave now!" Scrooge said, holding the thug's hands down and looking into his bloodshot eyes.

"You joined the wrong side, mate!" the thug said, his face inches from Scrooge's.

"No," said Scrooge, gripping the thug's wrists and staring into his eyes. "It's you who are on the wrong side."

They were interrupted by the voice of Bobbi Cratchit. "Jesu's bleeding."

Scrooge turned his head, and it was enough for the man to throw him off and stagger to his feet. Suddenly, the air was filled with the wail of a police siren.

"Leg it!" the cry rang out, as in the distance came the flashing blue and red lights of a police car. The other attackers needed no prompting, and with a final sneer at Scrooge, the tattooed man picked up his stiletto. "I'll be back for you!" he said as he hobbled away. But he walked straight into the arms of the two policemen who had rounded the corner of Scrooge Towers in pursuit of Scrooge. His stiletto was taken as he was grappled to the ground while his fellow attackers were chased by the police car that passed the front of the building, its siren blaring. And Scrooge turned as he heard Bobbi's voice, to see a sight that made his blood run cold.

81

"He's bleeding here," Bobbi said, pointing to Jesu's side where a red patch was spreading on his tattered shirt like a blossoming flower.

"My son," said Scrooge, dropping to his knee and taking Jesu's quivering body in his arms. "Son," he said, his eyes searching Jesu's but his eyelids had closed over. "Wake up, son," Scrooge said softly but urgently. Jesu's long eyelashes fluttered open, and his pupils focused on Ebenezer Scrooge.

"Pai?" he said uncertainly. Scrooge shook his head as tears pooled in his eyes and spilled down his face.

"I'm not worthy to be called father," he said, his voice cracking. He looked deep into Jesu's eye. Another police car skidded to a halt before them, but the background noise faded, and Scrooge found himself holding his son as if he was the only thing alive in the world.

He touched the hollowed face and bruised lips tenderly with his fingers, over the dried blood that caked Jesu's lips and the blue line of bruises. But Jesu smiled and, searching with his hand, found Ebenezer's and grasped it with surprising strength.

"Eu encontrei você – I found you," Jesu said, then his eyes flinched as if shot through with pain.

"Quiet, my boy," Scrooge said through the tears that were now falling freely down his cheeks. "Don't speak..." and he clasped the body of his son close to him, willing him to live.

His body was so frail, so young and he realised that Jesu was hardly more than a boy. He looked into Jesu's face and saw that his eyes were losing their focus, and they fluttered closed. And Ebenezer Scrooge, tightening his arms around Jesu, said, "Come back, son! Come back!" His voice was suddenly filled with authority, and with a jolt, Jesu opened his eyes and looked at the man holding him. In the distance was the wail of an ambulance. "They're on their way!"

Scrooge blinked away the tears as he tightened his grip on his son. "You are not to go – do you hear me?" The lion mane of hair nodded almost imperceptibly. "You are to stay here with me!" He laid the side of his face against the bloody, bruised face of his son as he whispered, "I love you."

And with those words, Jesu's eyes opened and he looked deep into the eyes of Ebenezer Scrooge, and nodded. "Te amo, Papai."

82

At the immigration desk of London Airport, Belle Santiago offered up a prayer as she waited in line. "Please don't let them arrest me and throw me in prison."

An old Jewish man wearing a kippah was being interviewed by the female officer in front of her and for a full minute Belle tried to deep breathe and control her nerves. She saw him leave and went up to the counter, feeling her heart pounding in her chest. Would the curse of Scorpius Scrooge follow her all the way to London? Would his threats that she would be arrested come true? She was about to find out as she stood in front of the biometric instrument that would reveal her true identity. "Please remove your glasses," the officer said curtly. This was not a good beginning, Belle thought. There was a long pause as Belle gazed deep into the hidden eye and she had the certain feeling that her identity would be exposed and she would be arrested. Then something happened. She saw a speck of light blink once in the depths of the scanner, a speck that reminded her of the strange shard of light that had hovered over her flat in favela and led her all the way from Rio de

Janeiro to London. At this sight, Belle felt a sudden jolt of reassurance and smiled. The officer looked up at her and after a moment's hesitation, she smiled back and waved her through with the words "Have a nice stay."

Once outside, Belle let out a long breath and stood for a moment, offering up a prayer of thanks. She was through and could now look for Jesu! She looked up at the sky for the shard of light but grey clouds hung over London for as far as the eye could see, disgorging snow.

"Jesu," she whispered in quiet desperation. She hailed a taxi and got in.

"Where to, ma'am?"

"The River Thames."

A perplexed look crossed the driver's face. "Where?"

"Just drive towards the river," she said with an urgency that made the driver turn and start the car. "It will come," she said to herself as they left the apron of the terminal and headed towards London. "The sign will come!"

But as they drove on, the clouds above grew darker and heavier as the snow fell and no shard of light was revealed to Belle Santiago's desperate eyes. That was until they reached the embankment at Victoria and Belle saw in the far distance a majestic dome and above it a pinprick of diamond light. "What is that building?" she asked the driver, leaning forward and pointing.

"St Paul's Cathedral, ma'am."

"There, drive there!" she said, her whole body alive with hope. And as she sat forward, willing the traffic to part and let them through, she thought she heard the voice of her son calling out to her. "Mamãe!" it whispered, from a long way off and desperate. "Mamãe!" And Belle Santiago stifled a sob.

83

On the cold quayside, Ebenezer Scrooge held his son and rocked him backwards and forwards like a baby. "I have found you!" he whispered, his voice caressing the air. "I have found you."

Jesu looked up at him with his clear blue eyes but they had a far-off look, as if he saw something that Scrooge could not. Then his whole body stiffened. "Mamãe!" he said, trying suddenly to sit up.

"What is it Jesu?" Scrooge said, following his son's eyes as they searched the road. A taxi skidded to a halt behind them and Scrooge turned and looked.

"Belle," he whispered. And in a flash, she was by his side, her face tear-stained as she took her son's hand in hers.

"Querida," she said, "my dearest."

And Jesu turned to her and for the first time in a long time, his gaunt face lit up.

"Mama," he said, "Eu vi você chegando!" He pulled his mother towards him in a hug. "Eu vi você chegando!" he said, the tears flowing down his face.

"What did he say?" Scrooge asked.

"He said he saw me coming!"

"Yes, he sat up – he knew," said Scrooge, feeling the strangest sensation as he looked at his son in his mother's arms. One of excitement mixed with joy. The sound of the ambulance's siren split the air as it braked to a halt and in seconds, careful hands were picking up Jesu. He was lifted and placed in the back of the ambulance.

It was the same crew who had visited Scrooge Towers just the day before and they looked at Scrooge and Bobbi Cratchit in wonder. "Any family members?" the ambulance driver asked.

"Yes!" both Belle and Scrooge said at exactly the same time. "You sure?" the ambulance driver blurted out, his only memory that of the cold and severe Ebenezer Scrooge from twenty-four hours ago.

"Yes!" said Scrooge and Belle again at the same time, with Scrooge offering Belle his hand as she clambered aboard. And they both allowed themselves the luxury of a smile as they sat in the ambulance beside their son, Belle not letting go of her son's hand as the doors closed and the siren wailed and they made their way to the hospital.

Part 6 –
The Reckoning

84

Ebenezer Scrooge was waiting on the doorsteps of his palatial home; his foot was tapping out an impatient, staccato rhythm on the floor. Scrooge glanced over at the graveyard, the scene of such commotion just a week ago, and his eyes searched the shadows. He had seen nothing of his father since that dramatic Christmas night and felt a stab of pain every time he thought of Scorpius's agony. "Father, where are you?" he whispered.

Car headlights appeared coming up the driveway, pulling Scrooge back from his thoughts as a car swept to a halt and a door opened. Out tumbled a gaggle of kids, with Fred and Donna following in the rear. Fred's children went immediately quiet on seeing Scrooge and stood in line as Fred approached and held out his hand.

"See, Uncle, you still have that effect on people!" He laughed but this time Scrooge took Fred's hand in both of his and shook it warmly.

"Hopefully that's changed," Scrooge said. He stood facing Donna and they both did a nervous dance, going from shaking hands to embracing rather stiffly to giving each other awkward kisses on the cheek.

"Well, Mr Scrooge," said Donna, covering her embarrassment, "I'm very happy to see you."

Scrooge held her in his stare, remembering the conversation he had overheard in her house with the Ghost. "You sure?" he asked.

Donna looked suddenly flustered. "Yes," she said uncertainly, then after glancing at her husband, she looked Ebenezer Scrooge in the eye. "I hear you've changed and I welcome that but—"

"Dear—" Fred went to intercede but Scrooge held up a hand.

"Your wife's quite right, Fred – I've been an absolute idiot and it's no wonder your kids are scared of me." He looked at the line of children who began to giggle nervously. "But time will tell and I thank you for coming from the bottom of my heart." He took both of Donna's hands. "And a big thank you to you, Donna – I know how difficult this visit is."

And Donna held his stare, intuiting that Uncle Scrooge had indeed changed. She nodded and began ushering her kids ahead of her, like a hen chasing her brood, leaving "Uncle Scrooge" with her husband.

Fred let out a long whistle. "*Pff* – that was nearly awkward."

"What do you expect, Fred?" Scrooge said, turning to his nephew. "I don't show up for years and suddenly overnight I'm a changed man." He laid a hand on Fred's shoulder. "I would be doubtful myself."

"What exactly happened, Uncle?"

"I got a second chance, Fred."

Fred smiled. "I'll take that!" he said and placed an arm around his uncle. "Does that mean you won't kick me out when I come calling at your office next Christmas?"

"It does indeed, Fred," Scrooge said, "and thank you for sticking with me for all those years." And they embraced warmly.

"Heh, Uncle, I bought you something," Fred said, digging deep into his pocket and handing Scrooge a small box wrapped in tissue paper. Scrooge opened the small black box and let out a stifled laugh.

"My goodness, Fred, where did you find this?"

"Looked away in the attic. You never know, it may come in handy."

Scrooge embraced his nephew again, holding him tight to his chest. "Thank you, Fred – thank you."

"I'll go and catch the brats," Fred said, "they're probably causing mayhem!"

But Scrooge caught him by the arm. "I'm sorry for ever calling them that word."

"What?"

"They're not brats — they're angels." And there was something so powerful in the way Scrooge spoke that tears filled Fred's eyes.

"They are indeed." And giving a final squeeze to his uncle's arm, Fred went inside.

85

Another set of headlights lit up the front of the house, and a battered old VW van wheezed to a halt in front of Scrooge. Seconds later, Doctor Ellie and a small group of homeless clients and volunteers stood before Ebenezer Scrooge.

Doctor Ellie bundled herself up the stairs, a riot of bright orange scarves and a red and brown voluminous skirt. She stopped and looked Scrooge right in the eye. "To be honest, it took a bit of persuading for me to come, Mr Scrooge!" she said.

"I'm not surprised, Doctor Ellie," Scrooge said, "and thank you for coming."

Doctor Ellie looked at Scrooge closely and leaned in to him whispering, "They say that you've gone and changed."

Scrooge leaned forward himself. "Who's 'they'?"

"Ah, people and things."

"People and things," Scrooge repeated, "and spirits?"

Doctor Ellie's expression became serious, and her eyes searched his face. "Whaddya mean?"

Scrooge looked at her face and remembered the shining light that had transformed her on that bitterly cold night on the waste ground. "You are alive inside – filled with light."

And Doctor Ellie's eyes widened, for she suddenly understood. "So they were right," she whispered, her voice filled with awe.

"I guess so," said Scrooge, laying a gentle hand on hers. She took it and held it as if weighing it, and her pupils dilated.

"Holy moly!" she said, a smile lighting up her face. "You're going to do powerful work, Mr Scrooge!"

"You think?"

"I know, sir."

"Good, well that powerful work will start with you."

"Are you serious?" she said, her eyes never leaving his.

"Deadly serious."

"Good," she said, squeezing his hand. She turned back to her group.

"I'm sorry but we're a bit light on numbers, Ebenezer," she wheezed, her large smile illuminated by a glittering set of white teeth. "Some of them folk are just not comfortable leaving their familiar spaces," she said, lowering her voice and nodding at the handful of homeless clients looking uncomfortably at the huge house that loomed over them.

Scrooge nodded and stood forward to welcome the group. "I'd like to particularly welcome you all here tonight. Please consider my house your home."

The group did not respond but rather shuffled up the steps guided by Doctor Ellie and her volunteers. Scrooge caught the eye of the young girl he had seen that night on the wasteland; the young girl that had sprouted angel wings. He looked at her with reverence and nodded as she looked back at him. Her eyes widened and for a split second, Scrooge saw, or imagined he saw, a white flash of light that lit up her whole countenance. Then she turned and was gone.

86

Scrooge resumed his vigil. The clock on the church tower struck 7 p.m. and again Scrooge found his eyes searching the graveyard lost in shadows as his lips mouthed the word "Father."

The final strike of the bell echoed across to where Scrooge was standing and a movement caught his eye. A circling movement almost too quick to follow. And there it was, settling on the spire of the old church, the peregrine falcon! Scrooge had noticed it from the first day after he had "returned" from his journey. And its presence had somehow offered Scrooge solace, offering a concrete connection with the other world that he had visited. And the bird's arrival heralded the entrance of two powerful headlights coming up the driveway, headlights so strong they made Scrooge shield his eyes. A large limo came to a graceful halt before him. Old George got out and, doffing his cap towards Scrooge, went round and opened the door.

Scrooge hurried down and wrapped Bobbi Cratchit in a warm embrace. He then ruffled the hair of Tim, who nodded curtly before clasping his mother's hand.

"So good to see you!" Scrooge said, escorting her up the stairs by the arm. Bobbi looked years younger and a smile lit up her face. Her hair showed signs of having been cut and coloured, while she wore a new, smart outfit.

"You look fabulous, Bobbi," Scrooge said, as they came to the top of the stairs.

She smiled back. "Thank you. Have they arrived yet?"

"No, but the others are all inside. How's the boy?" Scrooge asked, addressing Tim.

"Okay," Tim said.

"He's been through a lot," she said, her voice low, as he pulled Tim into an embrace.

"We all have," said Scrooge. There was the sound of crunching gravel as the limo pulled away, and Scrooge waved at the old chauffeur.

"George is in great form," said Bobbi. "I thought he'd retired."

"He had," said Scrooge. "But I asked him back for one last job."

Bobbi turned and looked at Scrooge closely. "And how are you, Ebenezer?"

Scrooge let out a mirthless laugh. "Getting there," he said. His eyes were drawn back to the graveyard, where they lingered.

"No sign yet?" said Bobbi.

Scrooge shook his head. "No."

"You'll hear something."

"Hope so."

There was the sound of another set of wheels on gravel and they turned to see an ambulance trundling down the driveway.

"Ah, here they come at last," said Scrooge as he bent down to speak to Tim. "Fred's kids are inside, Tim, they're looking forward to seeing you."

A shy smile appeared on Tim's face and he took his mum's hand and went inside while Scrooge jogged down the steps.

87

The ambulance doors were opened and the ambulance men helped Belle down and then lifted a gurney onto the driveway. Scrooge came forward and, leaning over Jesu, embraced his son gently.

"Como você está se sentindo meu filho?" Scrooge said. He had been practising his Portuguese and had had a new phrase ready for each day that he had visited his son in hospital.

"Good, Pai," Jesu said, taking his father's hand. He too had been practising English until the bout of pneumonia had hit. It was on day two of his hospital admission and it had put his life at risk, more than the stab wound that had turned out to be merely a superficial cut. A night in the Intensive Care Unit had followed, with both Belle and Scrooge keeping a ceaseless vigil. And in the moments when Jesu was sleeping, the two had caught up with their twenty years of enforced absence. And it took all of the three days and the rest of the week before they were abreast with what had happened.

Belle had told Scrooge about the terrible early days in Rio, trying to raise Jesu with only the help of her brother. "And all the time I thought that Scorpius would set the police on us and have us arrested!" And they had embraced and Scrooge had held her close as she went on to describe how Jesu fell into a deep despondency when he discovered that he had no father and ended up rebellious and in bad company. "He was arrested for using drugs and then he—" Belle broke down. "He tried to take his own life."

Scrooge had held her close as she told him about the two attempts Jesu had made on his life. "Eventually I had to tell him part of the story – that I had been forced to leave London and you because of the police. But he never accepted that. He stole the money to buy an air ticket to London and he left. No note. No nothing. And he had little or no money to live on and that soon ran out. He was homeless, a vagrant but he never gave up even at the end when he phoned me."

"I remember that," said Scrooge, as the memory of Jesu talking on Doctor Ellie's phone came back.

"Yes," continued Belle, "he never gave up the hope that he would find you."

"Did he even know my name?" Scrooge asked, looking into Belle's eyes and seeing for the first time the suffering she had endured.

"No! I could never reveal that – not after your father's threats."

"So he came looking for me but with no idea of my name or where I lived?"

Belle nodded. "Just the locket." She glanced down at Jesu's hand, lying on the hospital bed, a glint of silver between the fingers. "He never lets it go – it's his guiding light. Well, that and the light that actually guided both of us here." And Belle looked at him with eyes that glowed.

"I never saw that light," said Scrooge, looking in wonder at Belle and then his son. "But it led him to me. What was it?"

Belle shook her head. "I don't know but I bless it."

88

And Belle's confession prompted Scrooge to try to tell her about his own incredible journey but he struggled because he was heartbroken to think of his father's enduring suffering. "I can't bear to think of him alone while we are together." And Belle had placed a gentle finger on his lips. "The time will come when you can."

"You think so?" said Scrooge doubtfully.

She nodded and kissed his cheek and he embraced her, feeling her warmth and the sweet smell of her perfume. And that in itself had been healing. But still Scrooge thought of his father and the terrible fate that had awaited him. And his heart was heavy even though great changes were afoot, great changes that he was about to announce.

89

The week in hospital had gone well and resulted in Jesu's discharge. They had wheeled the gurney from the ambulance up to the house and willing hands soon had Jesu installed in the large front room, where he was tucked up on a leather Chesterfield couch, in front of a blazing fire and looking up in wonder at the largest Christmas tree he ever seen, while the company gathered around to celebrate his return to the bosom of his long-lost family.

The room was full of fun and life (a first in this household) with kids playing, friends chatting, while others sat in wonder at the fantastical Christmas decorations. For the giant Christmas tree was just the start of the merriment. There were flashing Christmas lights and decorations of every kind; so much so that Fred's kids, who had a high expectation of what a *real* Christmas should look like, were more than impressed. And the food and drink flowed. Mince pies and mulled wine for the adults and homemade cranberry soda and chocolate Yuletide logs for the kids. Plus, an endless supply of Christmas crackers that had the young ones telling terrible jokes while forcing all the adults in the room to wear brightly coloured paper hats. And it was here the homeless contingent found their tribe, led by Tim, who seemed to have an easy affinity. Soon they were playing Christmas games of Hide & Go Seek, or throwing dice as they chased snakes up ladders and down again.

"He's a natural!" beamed Doctor Ellie to Bobbi, who looked with pride at her son, who was holding the hand of the old woman with no teeth while showing her how to throw dice.

Finally, it was Scrooge who drew quiet from the chaos, as bubbling Champagne glasses were handed out to the adults and sparkling lemonade to the kids and their newfound friends.

"First," said Scrooge, "I want to thank you all for coming and I promise I will be brief!" This was met with murmurs of approval.

"You don't need me to tell you how awful a person I have been to" – he paused and looked around the room – "basically all of you. But maybe things have changed." He raised both arms up to the heavens. "I have changed. There, I said it!" And there were whoops of delight and the clapping of hands.

"So as part of this change, I have some announcements to make." There was a general murmur of excitement that Scrooge hushed with a calming gesture of his hand.

"First, I must mention the incredible Doctor Ellie and her team! She came to me asking for a donation and I sent her away empty-handed. And for that, I apologise."

"Apology accepted," said Doctor Ellie, her face beaming.

"But an apology is not enough." Scrooge reached into his jacket pocket and, taking out an envelope, walked over and handed it to her. More whoops and hollers greeted this as Doctor Ellie looked up at Scrooge. "Can I open this?"

"If you wish."

A hush fell on the gathering as Doctor Ellie tore open the envelope and took out a piece of paper. "It's a bank draft," she said. As she read it, she clamped a hand to her mouth. "You can't be serious, Ebenezer?"

She showed the draft to her two volunteers, who let out shrieks of disbelief.

"I am serious, Doctor Ellie, and there are a great many back payments included in that." The doctor was hugged first by Scrooge and then by her colleagues as Scrooge turned to Fred and his enormous family.

"Dear Fred, I apologise to you and your amazing family for twenty years of neglect."

"Ha, Uncle, we don't need an apology."
"I know that," Scrooge said, and, producing two sets of keys, he went over and handed one to Fred and the other to Donna.

"What are these, Uncle?"

"Keys to your new home."

"No, Uncle—"

"Yes, Fred. I calculated the cost of twenty years of Christmas presents for all of you, birthday presents, Christening presents and I worked it out that it would come to the cost of a house. So I bought you one."

"What?" asked Donna in disbelief. "Where?".

"Actually, it's just over the road. The old lady wanted to downsize so I made her an offer." All eyes looked through Scrooge's front window and gazed at the huge mansion facing them with a SOLD sign in the massive front garden. "And kids, it has a pool and tennis court so you can play."

The kids hurried over to the window. "Come back here this instant!" Donna cried angrily but Scrooge interrupted.

"Let them go, Donna, it's theirs!"

The kids gathered around their mother, who held the keys tight in her hand.

"Don't worry, dear," Fred said, pushing himself up off the sofa. "I'll go over with them."

"If you're going, we're all going!" Donna said, heaving herself up and joining the excited pack of kids.

"The interior designers are still working on it but it's nearly ready," Scrooge said as the small army of Fred and family disappeared and were soon seen racing down the driveway to their new home but not before Donna had taken Scrooge's hand and said, "The gift is great but greater still is the fact that Fred has his uncle back!" And she reached up and gave Scrooge a peck on the cheek.

90

When they had left, Scrooge turned to Bobbi, who was sitting across on a sofa, Tim snug by her side. Scrooge walked over and kneeled in front of her. "What I owe you, Bobbi, is beyond words."

Bobbi went to shake her head but Scrooge took her hand in his. "I literally owe you my life and so do my son Jesu and Belle."

Across the room, Belle put a hand on her heart and nodded over to Bobbi, while Jesu spoke in a voice filled with emotion, his mother translating as he went along.

"Estou aqui por causa da sua bravura, Bobbi . . . I am here because of your bravery. You saved my life not once but twice, when no one else cared. I have never, ever met anyone braver."

Bobbi fought back tears as they chinked glasses, and Scrooge returned to the centre of the room. "I have an announcement to make." The room went quiet. "I have wound up my company and fired myself as CEO." There were gasps of surprise before Scrooge continued. "I was a terrible boss, but I have set up a new company that will be dedicated to spending my fortune on helping people in need."

There was a chorus of approval. "But I need a new CEO," said Scrooge, "for I have other plans on how I want to spend the rest of my life." And as he said this, he looked over at Belle, who blushed and leant her head on her son's chest. "So," continued Scrooge, looking around the room till his eyes came to rest on Bobbi. "Will you run my new company?"

"I'm not qualified—"

"Can I be the judge of that, Bobbi?" And Scrooge walked over and offered his hand. "Deal?"

Bobbi looked at her son who nodded his approval, and reaching out, she took the hand of Ebenezer Scrooge. "Deal!"

91

As midnight approached, the party began to break up. Fred's kids had returned but were refusing to go back to their old home and eventually a compromise was reached. They would remain in Scrooge's vast mansion overnight and after breakfast go over and start moving into their new home.

Doctor Ellie left with her gang and her huge pay cheque safely stored in her handbag, which she thrust under her arm.

"The devil himself isn't getting his hands on this! Come on, gang, let's get going and leave Ebenezer and his family in peace. Come on now, the bus is leaving!" Doctor Ellie clucked like a mother hen. The last person out was the young girl with the needle marks on her arms. The girl who had sprouted angel wings when Scrooge had seen her through the shower of petals sprinkled by the Ghost. This same girl, still dressed only in a skimpy, soiled T-shirt and jeans, stopped in front of Scrooge, and looked up into his face.

"And angels walk amongst us unannounced," Scrooge whispered, recalling the words of the Ghost. And she had held him in her gaze with eyes that sparkled.

"Keep hoping and it will happen," she said mysteriously and reaching him, she kissed him on the cheek.

Finally, it was only Bobbi left with Tim fast asleep on the couch. Scrooge lifted the sleeping child and, with the help of George, laid him in the back of the Mercedes Benz.

"I'll see you on Monday," Scrooge said, holding both her hands in his. Scrooge went to the driver's side where George had lowered his window. "You'll see them home safely, George."

"Of course, sir," said George, preparing to start the car. "One last thing, George," said Scrooge as he fished something out of his pocket. "Here are the keys to the Ponton and may you have many happy years restoring the car to its glory!"

"You're joking, sir?" George said with uncertainty.

"No, George." He took an envelope from his jacket pocket and handed it to the old chauffeur. "A little something to help with the restoration." George took the envelope and looked inside. It was bulging with crisp, new £100 notes.

"This is too much, sir," he stammered.

"No, it isn't! Consider it a thank you for your fifty years of service, George," Scrooge said, and he bent down so his eyes were on the same level as the old man. "You have served my family well."

"A pleasure, sir," George said, saluting the rim of his chauffeur's peaked cap. "A pleasure."

Scrooge stood aside and waved to Bobbi, who had Tim asleep on her lap, only stepping back inside when the car had disappeared from view.

92

Scrooge returned to Belle and Jesu, who were snuggled up on the Chesterfield sofa.

"Son, you'll be more comfortable upstairs."

But Jesu shook his head. "No, Papa! Estou feliz aqui – I'm comfy here with my family."

And Scrooge knelt by his son. "I was very nearly responsible for your death, Jesu, and for that I can hardly forgive myself. But I must and I will."

"Why must you, Papa?" Jesu asked, looking amused at his father's sudden seriousness.

"My father came back to say he was sorry and offered me another chance." Scrooge squeezed Jesu's hand. "And when I discovered that you were my son, I realised that I had treated you exactly as he had treated me. I nearly killed you. I was no better than him."

"You didn't know I was your son."

"It didn't matter – everyone deserves respect."

"And did you forgive your father – my grandfather?"

Scrooge smiled. "Never thought of him as that but yes, I did forgive your grandfather!" And Scrooge looked at Jesu. "Can you forgive me?"

Jesu gently cupped his father's face. "There is nothing to forgive, Papa." And Jesu kissed the forehead of his father. Ebenezer Scrooge buried his head in his son's arms and finally let out the cry of anguish and the tears of sadness that had been building since the day of his birth.

93

When Jesu had finally fallen asleep, Scrooge looked at Belle.

"Come, let's take some air," she said.

They stood on the front step and Belle took his hand as they stood looking at the church.

"That's where it all began?" she said softly.

"Yes, where it all began," said Scrooge, as he searched for something in his pocket. "Look what Fred found!" he said, handing the small box to Belle. She opened it and let out a gasp.

"Our rings! How did he find them?"

She held the ring up to the light. Scrooge held his wedding ring up beside Belle's, gold against gold.

"Fred was the groom's boy, remember?"

Belle's large brown oval eyes looked at the rings in wonder. "Yes, I remember, he was a child." Then her face took on a troubled look. "All those wasted years."

"We can reclaim those years," he said, looking into Belle's eyes.

"How?"

"By picking up where we left off."

"What do you mean, Ebby?"

"Let's get married."

"Are you serious?"

"Never more serious in my life." They embraced and Scrooge could feel her warmth, the old warmth that had comforted and excited him then as it did now. The warmth that made him come alive. He took Belle's wedding ring and held it just above her wedding finger. "Belle, will you marry me?"

94

Belle's eyes moistened and she returned his passionate stare. "Yes, Ebenezer Scrooge, I will marry you!" And they kissed long and passionately. And for Scrooge it was an awakening of a passion that had slumbered long, even to the point of dying, but by some miracle had returned to reignite again and burn bright.

They broke off their kiss and stood looking at one another and Belle's eyes crinkled in a smile. "Only one thing, Ebby."

"Yes?" said Scrooge.

"Your father must *not* make an appearance at the wedding!"

They embraced again, laughing, and Scrooge looked over the shoulder of his wife-to-be and his eyes rested on the graveyard. Suddenly, his whole body stiffened.

95

Suspended mid-air was Scorpius Scrooge, but not as his son had ever seen him. He was covered in light. And his father beckoned to him and Scrooge felt a sudden surge of joy.

"I'm coming, Dad!" he said, and there was a *plop* as his spirit shot out of his body like a cork from a Champagne bottle. Scrooge found himself back in the strange and familiar world where spirits roam and time stands still. And he felt again the strange sensation of being a spirit in human form; of being able to look down on his body wrapped in Belle's arms, while at the same time approaching the spectre of his father. And as he got closer, he saw that Scorpius was utterly changed. He was clothed in the light, the same light that he had seen emanating from the girl who had been transformed into an angel. And Scrooge understood what she had meant when she had whispered in his ear: *Keep hoping and it will happen.*

And it had happened.

As he got closer, Scrooge saw that his father was standing in a column of light. And looking up, he saw that the column came from the shard that he had seen over London. The shard that had guided him and the others. The shard that had protected them all. And Scrooge arrived in front of his father and looked at him in wonder. "What happened, Father?" he said.

"Son, I have been given leave to come to you one last time," Scorpius said. His voice was no longer tortured and strained, but soft and melodic, like music. "Your forgiveness released me from my torment. And I am now free to return to the light!"

"And your chains?" said Scrooge, searching for them on his father's body as Scorpius's face broke into a smile.

"I cast them away."

There was a pulse of light and the luminous tunnel that connected him to the heavens opened and Scrooge looked up in wonder.

"I have to go, son," said Scorpius, and there was an excitement to his father's voice that Scrooge had never heard before.

"Where are you going?"

"Home."

"Home?" Scrooge said, feeling a sudden stab of pain in his heart. "No, Father!"

"Yes, son, and know this: your love saved me." And slowly the spirit of Scorpius Scrooge began to ascend.

"No, not yet!" cried Scrooge. "I just got you back. You can't leave!" And as he looked at his father, Scrooge felt something ignite inside. "Father, I love you."

"My dearest son," Scorpius said. "We have found each other; we are never apart." And he reached out a hand and placed it on Scrooge's head. "Go and enjoy at last the love of your wife and the love of your son." Scorpius's eyes began to fill with the same light as the tunnel. "And tell Jesu I will be watching over him, for he is my grandson." Tears sprang to the eyes of Scorpius Scrooge, tears of light as he clasped his son to him. And Ebenezer Scrooge surrendered to the love of his father for the very first time in his life and he felt something shift deep inside. When Scorpius let him go, Scrooge felt a lightness, as if a great weight had been lifted. And he knew, in that moment, that he had been healed.

"Will I see you again?" Scrooge asked as his father began to ascend.

"Oh yes, son." And his voice was subsumed into the sound of laughter and music suddenly filled the air above. Scrooge watched his father, Scorpius Scrooge, far, far above, being welcomed into a land of light. And as he disappeared from sight, Scrooge let out a cry.

A woman had come to greet Scorpius, and in that instant Scrooge saw for the first time his mother truly alive and filled with light. "Mother!" he whispered, and she looked down on him and smiled, and Scrooge felt petals of light fall from her and descend around his head before the tunnel finally closed over and the shard disappeared.

96

"What is it, Ebby?" Belle said. She was searching Scrooge's eyes as he suddenly returned to his body. Scrooge took a deep breath as he felt the solid ground under his feet.

He looked at Belle and leant his forehead against hers. But her voice sounded troubled as she asked, "Are you okay, my love?"

Scrooge nodded, sighing. "Yes, I am and there's good news."

"What's that?" said Belle.

"Well," he said, holding her in a close embrace, "you'll be glad to know that my father won't be attending our wedding!"

"How would you know that?"

"I just met him."

He felt her laughter as she gently shook in his arms. "Ebenezer Scrooge, you are one of a kind."

And as he nestled his head on hers, he heard a cry and, looking up, saw the peregrine falcon alight from the church spire and circle up towards the sky in what looked like a flight of pure joy. Scrooge led Belle back into his house where his son, and family and friends were sleeping.

And as he turned to look one last time at the church and the graveyard beyond, he saw that his hand was glowing and holding it closer, he saw one last petal of light shining before it was absorbed into his being. Ebenezer Scrooge felt a shiver of excitement as the realisation dawned that he was loved beyond his imagining, both by those alive and those who were dead.

"Thank you," he said, before he closed the door. "Thank you!"

THE END

Printed in Great Britain
by Amazon